Airship 27 Productions

An Airship 27 Production
www.airship27.com
www.airship27hangar.com

Cover illustration © 2022 Chris Kohler
Interior illustrations ©2020-2022 Rob Davis

Editor: Ron Fortier
Associate Editor: Rob Davis
Marketing and promotion: Michael Vance
Production designer Rob Davis.

ISBN: 978-1-953589-41-5

Printed in the United States of America

10 9 8 7 6 5 4 3 2 1

Greg Hatcher's Dr. Fixit

INTRODUCTION

Dear Reader,

I met Greg in the fall of 1998. He was teaching a class of elementary to middle school kids about cartooning at the Alki Bathhouse art studio. I knew the first day I met him that he was someone I wanted to get to know. He looked like he'd be a good friend. After building a friendship with him for over five years and dating for one, he proposed. That was 18 years ago.

Greg wrote about everything; our story, his work, and his life before "us." He wore many hats; at WITH Magazine he was a writer, editor, and illustrator for the pop culture and fiction stories, at Comic Book Resources he was a writer and a moderator, and at The Atomic Junkshop, which he founded with long-time friend Jim MacQuarrie, he was one of the main writers. During this time he also wrote for Airship27, which he enjoyed immensely.

Dr. Fixit is known for his power to fix and to make, wanted by those both good and evil. He suffers no fools and does his best to protect his family and the people around him. Not only did Greg enjoy creating and writing the character, but doing so helped him have the confidence to improve his mechanical skills. You see, Greg thought he flunked "guy school" because he didn't care for sports and his automatic approach to fixing things was using duct tape. Through writing Dr. Fixit, I think he realized that he didn't actually flunk "guy school." In fact, I think he realized a bit of his own potential through the character and this is what makes the writing so compelling.

Greg was and always will be my Dr. Fixit. He fought long and hard against the cancer that took his life, and just like the character, we used all the tools in the toolkit to try and save him. If you take one thing from Dr. Fixit, and from Greg's life, please use all the tools in your toolkit to keep yourself happy and healthy, and around for those who love you. The world is not the same without you in it.

Finally, I would be remiss not to thank Fred Adams Jr. for helping to finish the story, Chris Kohler for doing the cover, Captain Ron Fortier for editing this collection, and Chief Engineer Rob Davis for the wonderful illustrations throughout the book. And thanks to Rowan Hatcher, my editor, and our #1 Hatchling. It is thanks to this team, and many others, that we can now present these stories to the world. We hope these stories give you great joy, and that you love the adventure of it all.

Respectfully,

Julie M. Hatcher
Greg's Wife and #1 Fan

P.S. This isn't the end! Keep a look out for news of more of Greg's work to be published in the future!

HENCHING IT WITH DR. FIXIT

The first thing Christine Vance noticed about the old man in the wheelchair were his eyes. Despite the seamed face that was yellowed and liver-spotted with age, Ernie Voskovec's eyes were bright and blue and twinkling with good humor. When he spoke, his voice was wry with disdain, but she could hear the smile behind it.

"Lemme guess," he said. "This is another one of those *Whatever-Happened-To* things, right? Where is Captain Dynamo? Why'd he disappear after the fire? And so on. I already said my piece to all the TV and newspaper types years ago. Which one you with, honey?"

"NPR." At his baffled look, Christine added, "National Public Radio."

"Okay. Whatever." Voskovec shrugged. "It doesn't matter. I don't got anything to add." He added, "You been at this long? You look awful young. I mean at my age everybody looks like they're in effing kindergarten, but..."

"I'm twenty-two." Christine said. "I'm new, I admit it. I've been researching the St. Jacques City supers for a series my boss wants to do and I came across some old police reports about the Battle of Easter Sunday. Your name was there as one of the survivors. They listed you as a bystander but..."

"But?" The old man's head jerked up sharply.

Christine paused for a moment and then plunged ahead. "Well... the reports don't quite add up. There are discrepancies."

Voskovec rolled his eyes. "Another conspiracy nut. Everybody has their own pet theory about that night, about how Diamond Brain's still alive, or how Cap Dynamo was murdered and didn't just quit. You think I'm part of some scheme, right? I must get five or ten letters a week about that shit. Most folks think it was UFOs, or the Cubans what got Kennedy, or whatever."

"No, nothing like that." Christine paused again and then thought, *the hell with it. The worst he can do is yell for the nurse and send me away.* "What I mean is ... you worked for the Brain, didn't you?"

For a moment Voskovec looked like he might deny it, then he laughed. "Okay, blondie. You got me. I didn't think a cute young thing like you had any juice but you didn't get that from no clipping. Somebody must have talked. Who was it? Just curious."

"Danny Souchak over at the 57th just retired. He said I reminded him of his daughter. He was the desk officer on duty that night and he remembers how Cap brought you in and the big fight with the EMTs about where you were going." She paused again, not sure how to proceed.

Voskovec waited, not giving her any help.

Finally she said, "Souchak said Captain Dynamo said you weren't to be charged, that you were a hero. And that there was an argument but Cap won it, there were no charges, and your involvement got scrubbed from the reports. And that's all he would tell me. Anything more than that he said I'd have to ask you. And… here I am. Asking."

Voskovec considered it and nodded. "All right. You serious about this, girlie? You want to be a real reporter?"

Christine's smile was wan. "I do. Nobody thinks I can because I'm young and a girl and a blonde and, you know..."

"Stacked?" Christine flushed and Voskovec brayed with laughter. "Well, you are. I got eyes." He grew serious. "But you found Danny and you found me. I think you might have what it takes." He fell silent.

Christine waited, not daring to say anything.

Finally Voskovec snorted. "Sure, I'll tell you what happened. It's been, what, twenty years? Most everybody who was there is gone now. No harm to it. And people ought to know. Maybe it'll shut off them crackpot letters, getting the real story out there." He glanced at Christine. "Got your notebook ready, toots?"

She pulled a tape recorder out of her purse. Then she fished out a note pad and a ball-point pen, smiling up at Voskovec as she did so. "I would like to record this, but I'll also take notes. I just don't want to miss anything."

"Attagirl." Voskovec grinned back at her. "Professional. I knew you was the real thing. Okay, you ready?"

Christine nodded.

Voskovec settled back into his wheelchair and his eyes grew distant. "It was like this…"

•••

I started in the fifties, before it blew up into such a thing. Henching it.

For a while there in the fifties and sixties, it was almost like showbiz. Crime, but, y'know, performing too. Crazy costumes, theme robberies, big publicity. Lotta guys thought maybe the hero-villain thing was a fad, like a first step to TV or the movies. Never really worked for any of 'em but people kept trying. There was that Count Von Drache guy kept showing up on talk shows like Steve Allen, claiming to be psychic… he'd predict which bank was gonna get hit next. Turns out that his arch-enemy Black Wing hitting all them banks—it was *him*. Same guy, different suit. There was a lot of that kind of thing back then. Nutty, but kind of funny in a weird way. Nobody took it too serious. Not even cops. They used to be friendly with the supers, some of 'em anyway.

It wasn't like real crime. Real criminals don't screw around with costumes or making big pronouncements on pirate broadcasts or stuff like that. They just want money, lots of it, without a lot of drama. The real crooks in St. Jacques hated the supers but even more, they hated the super villains. If a hero-type like Liberty Jane breaks up your dockside smuggling operation, okay, that's a couple nights' work lost. But somebody like Preying Mantis moves in to a warehouse to start running his conquer-the-city mad-science routine there on the same wharf your dope import operation's on, that's just bad for business all around. Way too much noise and attention and it just keeps going till some vigilante comes and blows it all up.

These supervillain guys, they all needed crew. I started henching in '56—

What? 'Henching'? That's just what we called it. Press, they called us 'henchmen' and it sorta caught on, guys thought it was funny, see? We were already kind of laughing at the bosses behind their backs just because they were all so damn weird. Lizard King, he wanted his crew all in matching outfits like some kind of chorus line. Green shirts, black slacks, white ties. Really.

So we got to calling it henching. It was sorta code, like, for 'illegal but not too serious,' right? Most guys what got caught didn't even do real time. They'd already had their jaw dislocated or their leg broke by Captain Good-Guy whoever; that made the bust not so clean in the first place, so prosecutors mostly wanted them to flip on their bosses. Then the case could go to trial without a lot of vigilante crap getting in the way. It was easy to cut a deal.

I got into it because my wife Debbie, she was diagnosed with what turned out to be leukemia. They know a lot more about it today but then it was just test after test and doctor after doctor, no one of them really sure what to try next, and all our savings drying up. I'd heard about this bone marrow therapy but it was thousands of dollars, there was no way I'd be able to get that much cash together. You don't know desperate till you're in a fix like that, watching somebody you love maybe dying and knowing you can stop it if you can just get the money. I was an electrician but not union—union, I'd'a had insurance and none of this what you want to know about would have ever happened, probably.

I was always mechanical. Plus I had a little side business out of my garage, fixing up people's lawn mowers and cars and whatnot. Just always been good with machines really. So naturally I was on the lookout for more work like that and a buddy of mine, Travis, hits me up in the tavern one night, says he heard I was looking for some fast money. Might not be entirely legit, he says, kind of nervous-like. But mechanical, something in my line.

Turns out it was the Midnight Midas wanted his lair done. These guys all had their secret underground whatever with the big-screen monitors and the giant supercomputers and hidden entrances and whatnot. Well, they don't issue those along with your villain costume. Somebody's gotta build it. And even trickier, somebody's got to do the wiring for it. You seen pictures of those places, right? You must have if you're looking up stuff on the old supers. Big aluminum rooms full of cool gadgets, right? That shit is hard to wire up and Midas wanted it to *work* and he wanted there to be no sign of him using power off the city grid. Couple of his guys had already screwed the pooch trying to make it work and he got so goddam mad he shot the second one. *Get me a real honest-to-God electrician,* says Midas to his guys, and my pal Trav remembered me and my garage sideline. I was the best electrician and mechanic he knew and the job needed both.

Like I said, he pitched it to me kind of nervous—he says it would be big money, huge money, but it might be risky. Probably thinking of the guy what got shot. It didn't matter to me. I knew Trav was into some crooked shit, small-time; I already figured it was some kind of illegal thing but I just didn't care. Honestly by then I was so desperate I was lying awake at night wondering how hard it would be to rob a bank or something, and Debbie would get all weepy saying she wasn't worth me gambling my freedom like that.

But she was. She was the love of my life, kid, and I knew two things—I would do anything to get her well and I would make sure anything bad I had to do would never touch her.

So I said to Trav sure, I'll do it.

And it worked out very well for me. Turns out this was the job I was born to do.

Seriously. Supervillain lairs. Who knew? But I had a real knack for it, solving wiring problems and figuring out cooling systems for supercomputers and whatnot. Computers, you know, they're a lot smaller now, they look like frigging adding machines. But back then they were the size of a

VW bus and they ran hot, because they sucked so much power. That was another thing, hiding the power demands, because a smart cop could just read the meters in a neighborhood and figure out where Steel Spectre or whoever was headquartered.

God, I loved getting to play with all the toys. Lasers, rockets, mazes and death rays—just any cockamamie electrical or mechanical whiz-bang shit you could think up, I probably worked on it. You know those bastards at Kawasaki patented the Jet-Ski in '72 but I created almost the same damn thing for the Ocean Bandit's crew in 1959 for that shootout on Lake Mead. These guys spent money like water on the craziest goddam things. Most of 'em, they were just nuts in weird suits, they didn't really know what they were asking for half the time. I once got a three thousand dollar bonus for figuring out how to get a giant Jacob's Ladder in behind the throne looking out over Devilhound's control room. Hell, you probably don't even know what that is. It's two antennas that have these pulsing arcs of electricity shooting between 'em, you know, they don't *do* anything, the effect just looks cool. That's the kind of shit most of these guys wanted. It was all visuals with them.

But you want to hear about the Brain.

So it was about '68, thereabouts. I'd just said so long to a nice little gig setting up the catacombs for the Electric Ladyland Mob; they wanted me to be permanent but I could see they was going to crash hard and fast. Too many drugs and hippies in that outfit to go the distance. An off-duty cop with a couple of beers in him could have put that bunch away, it wouldn't take no super, so I just took my fee and said thank you very kindly and moved on.

I'd always been careful like that. I was getting a little bit of a rep myself by this time, some of the guys were calling me Doctor Fixit, and I'd put my pal Trav—remember him? The guy that put me on to Midas, way back when—he was on my payroll as a broker. And he comes in with this offer for what looked like another run-of-the-mill lair job. Guy had a warehouse property on the docks he wanted fitted out with camouflaged gun turrets and a submarine garage and secret entrances and the whole nine yards. I'd do one or two of those a year and that was more than enough to cover me and Debbie and even Trav's wages. Debbie was in a home by then, she was too sick to be on her own and I knew it was just a matter of time.

But what I didn't know—none of us that were henching for him really knew—was that Diamond Brain wasn't just another nut in a weird suit. He was the real thing. He had powers, he was a super himself, and he was stone crazy.

Here's the thing that never made it into the newspapers or the history books. You been researching so you probably know about the Liberty Formula, the serum that made all the supers in the first place. You might even know that government folks kept trying to duplicate it after the original formula and all the research went up in flames.

But it wasn't just government.

The mobs wanted in on it too. Mostly they'd get these sketchy doctor guys what had their medical license yanked or something like that and set 'em up in a lab someplace. Sometimes it was some grifter who pretended to be a chemical genius and sold himself to the local families as the guy who could give them super-powered guys to meet folks like Sergeant Smasher or Madame Justice on equal terms. None of it ever came to anything. Most of the time these idiots only managed to set themselves on fire or accidentally blow up their labs or whatever.

Except once. The one time it *worked* was Diamond Brain.

Who was he? You mean originally? Hell, I dunno. Nobody ever dared to talk about the before part of the before-and-after with him. I heard he was some small-timer working off a debt to Johnny Maguire, something to do with the Irish mob and horse doping. Something like that. But once they juiced him up—Jesus. His I.Q. was off the charts and he could look at you with those cobra's eyes of his and actually—I don't know the word. Like telepathy, but more like you had to do what he said. The guys henching for him called it the Push. It didn't always work; you kind of had to be already leaning that way. It wasn't like he could hypnotize a mother into drowning her baby or nothing like that. But if you were maybe thinking about spilling something to a cop, he'd know, and he'd make you stop wanting to do it. And if you tried to fight it you'd suddenly have the mother of all headaches.

It never worked on women. Just guys. Why, I don't know. But that was where the trouble really started, it was what sent the Brain over the edge. It was a woman. It's always a woman, really.

What? I don't mean that in a bad way, toots. Don't get me wrong. I respect women. Honest. I'm talking to you, ain't I? But you gotta understand—men, their brains just don't work when it comes to the women in their lives. Look at me. I got into this because of my Debbie. And the Brain—for Chrissake, he effing *owned* St. Jacques for a while there, he had all the mob families peeing their pants they was so scared of him. He coulda had his pick of women. There's always a babe that wants to get next to money and power. Don't look at me like that, you know it's true.

But the one he wanted, he couldn't have. So of course she was all he thought about. And that's where the trouble started.

Who was she? Her name was Amanda Harding. I bet you never found her name anywhere in those old clippings, right? She was a biology prof at SJU, the one what figured out the bootleg Liberty formula that made the Brain what he was. She was smart and funny and a hell of a looker on top of all of it. It's no wonder the Brain fell so hard. I think on some level he wanted a woman as smart as him just to have somebody to talk to—those girls that hang around mob guys aren't all that much between the ears, you know what I'm saying? Nobody keeps them around for their smarts.

But Amanda, she had smarts *and* looks. She tried to hide it, she had big horn-rimmed butterfly glasses and she kept her hair screwed down tight into a bun but she still had a whole sexy-librarian, smart-girl-gone-bad look to her.

Well, she mostly had smarts, but she was dumb about guys, or pretended to be—not sure which and it doesn't matter. Either she just plain didn't realize how bad the Brain had it for her or she was trying to be gentle about stiff-arming him. Either way, for her, he was just a subject. Lab rat, like. It wasn't till right at the end she even knew he was crooked, never mind him being the boss of bosses here in St. Jacques City.

I met her when I was doing a consult with Brain on the new lair. I'd been called in to the office—it was the upstairs office, the one in the dock-side warehouse façade. We were still doing finishing work on the underground part otherwise Brain never would have let himself be seen up there.

I got there a little early and I saw he had someone else in the office. I didn't want to interrupt—Brain was a little freaky about that, he didn't like people busting in on him. The door was open a little bit and I heard voices, so I stopped.

A woman's voice—this was Dr. Harding, though I didn't know her name at the time—was saying, "I don't know, Ronald. It has to be some kind of secondary chromosomal mutation. The dihymenidrol, even if it was accidentally irradiated as we discussed, shouldn't have affected you the way that it did. Justin reacted in a completely different way and his DNA is chained in almost exactly the same—"

"Must we talk about Justin?" The Brain's voice was still kind of hissing like always, but the tone—It was different. I'd never heard him like that before. Almost like pleading. Maybe that was why I hung back, listening, instead of high-tailing it like I should have.

The woman's voice again. "Whatever you think of him, he's still my patient, as are you. The two of you are the only link I have with my researches since the government shut down the program. You know what I'm up against. I'm blacklisted ever since the campus protest incident. I don't dare try to get in to see him at the lab. At least he lets me call on him at home, as you do." A pause. "I honestly don't understand the rift between you two. Of course he has had advantages you haven't but even so—"

"Let's not go through it all again." The Brain sounded tired all of a sudden. "Have you had a chance to look at the other material? The rhodopsin flasher?"

"I did, and it was fascinating reading." The woman's voice brightened, "I confess that theory had never occurred to me but I think you must have hit on it. It would explain both the need for eye contact and the gender differentials in the dysphasic side effects of…of what you can do. Your abilities are somehow tied up with the rhodopsin cycle, and your concept of a mechanical model is frankly beyond anything I've seen. It's cutting edge, and it could help so many people…"

"Then you will work with us on it?"

"Of course. But I don't have any grasp at all of the electronics, or the mechanical principles—"

"I have just the man to help with that." The Brain's voice raised a bit. "Join us, won't you, Ernie?"

I felt foolish, and a little jumpy at being caught listening. But there was no help for it, so I pushed the door open and went on in, nodding at both of them. "Boss. Ma'am."

"Hello, Ernie. This is Amanda Harding, she's a physician with expertise in radiation and neurology. Dr. Harding, this is Ernie Voskovec, our electronics expert." Brain was smiling, which was weird. He looked almost normal.

Then it hits me. He's trying to look all normal for this woman, he wants to make a good impression, like. Goddamnedest thing. He's got the whole city in the palm of his hand but he's looking at this woman like he's working up the nerve to ask her to the prom.

I'm sure not going to be the guy to screw that up for him. He wants to look like the big man here, I'll play my part. "Yes sir, and pleased to make your acquaintance as well, ma'am." I turned back to Brain. "What can I do for you?"

"I want you to look at these." Brain spread out a bunch of—well, not really blueprints but more like thumbnails, some of them just pencil sketches, some of them pasted together from circuit diagrams torn out of old copies of *Popular Mechanics* or something like that. At first glance it looked like a crazy kid's craft project.

I leaned in for a closer look. Suddenly it made sense. "This is—like a generator, you want to send a sonic pulse? Subsonic, I guess really. But I don't understand this part here... this isn't sound, this is a UHF circuit—"

"That's where the doctor comes in." Brain was rubbing his hands. "The idea is to find a frequency broadcast that resonates with the optic nerve, particularly the rhodopsin cycle that converts photons into a chemical signal to the neurons in the brain. Synaesthetic induction. You design a prototype mechanism based on the data she supplies you; that will give you the frequency ranges. Can it be done?"

"I can build it, sure." I was shaking my head. "But we'll have to machine a lot of this stuff on site, right here. I can't order parts for something like this out of a catalogue. This is going to take time."

"As long as you need. Just make it happen." Brain was grinning now, almost giddy. "You see, Doctor? We can manage without government sponsorship. Your work proceeds."

Dr. Harding narrowed her eyes a little, looking at me and then at the Brain. Something must have passed muster, because she gave a little brisk nod and said, "I suppose it does. Just... please bear in mind what I said earlier. We must go slowly. This is uncharted territory for all of us." She stood up. "I'll be in touch. Nice meeting you, Ernie."

I started to go too but Brain held up a hand. "Not just yet, Ernie. Stay a moment." When the door closed the smile disappeared and he was his usual scary-ass self again. I thought he was going to chew me out for eavesdropping earlier but instead he says, "This mechanism, the pulse generator. How large can we make it? To extend the range to... let's say five miles."

"A five-mile diameter you mean? Because honest to God, boss, I can't make this directional." I still couldn't figure out what he was getting at with this thing. "There's other problems too. The power demands—there's no way we can do it and stay underground. Our local generator can't handle it and if we tap the city grid that'll spike every needle they've got downtown. Might cause a brownout. Blackout even."

"It needn't be directional. It's not a cannon. It's a broadcast array. But I want it to dominate every radio and television in St. Jacques City when the time comes."

"Well—" I scratched my head. "Multi-frequency, multi-channel array... using these weird frequency pulses—how long you want it to go on? I can give you maybe two minutes at most before the whole thing flames out. And then we're down, the circuit's fried. Getting it up and running after that means we have to replace a lot of components by hand, one at a time. And the blowout's going to be like sending up a flare to the cops. We'd all be frog-marched into the paddy wagon before we even got a start on fixing it up to go again." I was talking more to myself now, scowling at the puzzle Brain had posed, trying to solve it.

Suddenly I had it. "Wait a minute. Hold the phone. I think I got it, boss. We got a submarine hangar, right? You have subs?"

Brain looked suddenly suspicious. "What matter of business is it of—"

"No, no, I don't care about that, I'm just saying, boss, that's how you solve the power problem. A sub has a nuclear reactor that's compact and designed to run on its own for years. We take it out of the sub and install it down below. We can run your rhodopsin broadcast widget off of that and have plenty left over for the rest of the installation here. All self-contained. Safe as houses." I was grinning myself now, all on fire with solving the problem and getting to build this thing. "We can do this."

Brain was nodding now, all caught up. "Well done, Ernie. All right then, let's do it. Get going."

That's always how it went for me in those days. Just figuring out the me-chanical stuff. It never even occurred to me to ask why the Brain wanted a machine that could broadcast a signal through the optic nerves of every citizen in St. Jacques City. Or what that signal would be.

●●●

Debbie was in a place called Resthaven. Not a lot different than this place, really, except the food was a little better. When I was done for the day I'd usually go sit with her for a while. Sometimes I'd stop and get her an éclair from the bakery down the street she liked. I mean, the docs were strict about her diet but an éclair was pretty tame, I didn't mind sneaking her in something fun like that. I think I knew she didn't have long. But I was gonna be with her as much as I could while I could.

But that night—after the meeting with Dr. Harding, I mean—I walk into the place with my bag of éclairs, same as always. The front desk lady knows me, of course, so I didn't stop to check in or nothing. But Debbie's not in her room.

Instead there's this tough guy with a crewcut and a gray suit. He holds out a leather card case but I already knew he was a Fed. "I'm Bud John-son," he says, and tucks the case back in his vest pocket after I nod at him. "You're Ernie Voskovec?"

"This is—like a generator, you want to send a sonic pulse?"

"Yeah." I glanced around. Everything's fine, all the stuff's where it should be. Just no Debbie. "Where's my wife?"

"Safe."

"Okay. But where?"

He ignored me and went on, "We need you to help us out, Mr. Voskovec."

"I need you to tell me where my wife is or I'm going to kick your ass. I ain't done nothing and neither has she. For Christ's sake, she's—"

He held up a hand. "Calm down. Your wife is fine. One of our girls is down in the cafeteria with her. She thinks we're from the hospital board and you're discussing a possible new treatment study. She doesn't know what you really do for money, does she, Voskovec?"

I just stood there for a second. Thinking *How much has he got? What's he want? Is it the Brain or something else?*

But he surprised me. "We are interested in a woman named Amanda Harding. I understand you might have some knowledge of her. It would appear she's engaged in some sort of agreement with the warehousing firm you are currently contracted with. What are you building down there, Mr. Voskovec? How is Dr. Harding involved?"

Now I was caught up. "You don't want me at all," I says to him. "Or her either. Not really. You want the Liberty serum. The supers formula."

Didn't faze him. "Of course we want it. It's ours. That's proprietary bio-technology she created in government service. She has no right to sell it to anyone."

I was getting mad again, and I could feel a headache coming on. "That ain't what she's doing at all. She's just tryin to help—" I stopped. I didn't want to tell him about the Brain. *Oh Jesus,* I thought. *The Push.* Brain Pushed me. Must have. My headache was getting worse. If I tried to go against it and spill on Brain I'd have a stroke.

Johnson saw me hesitate and must have thought I was worrying about consequences. He leaned forward. "I don't want to know what you've got going on down there, that's not my brief. You go ahead and run whatever smuggling scheme or whatever you've got going on. We're not the cops. But we need Harding and her formula. We need you to be a pipeline to her. Keep us posted. That's all. Once we bag her and whatever work stuff she has, notes, samples… then we'll relocate you and your wife. Full immunity deal. And your wife never needs to know you were a career criminal." His voice was low, persuasive.

"And if I say no?"

"You go to jail. It all comes out, every shitty thing you've ever done, every murdering freak you've ever abetted with your gadgets. Your wife stays right here and rots. Knowing her husband's a crook who contracts with killers and thieves."

What could I say? I sighed and spread my hands. "Okay. As long it's just Harding, right?" I had to struggle to get the words out. My head was pounding. "And full immunity."

"Absolutely." He nodded.

My headache faded a little. *Just Amanda, no threat to Brain*, I kept telling myself, trying to beat back the Push he'd given me. Even though I knew it was a lie, it helped a little.

He looked at me for a second and then one brisk nod, satisfied. He handed me a card and said, "Call us at that number when you hear something." He stood up. "Go see your wife. If we don't hear from you in a couple of days—"

"I'll call. You got me by the balls here. I don't have no choice."

Johnson looks at me again, with kind of a sad smile. "No. You really don't. But it's a good deal, Mr. Voskovec. Better than you deserve."

"What if I can't give you Harding?"

"You will." He shrugged. "Like you said. You have no choice."

•••

So now I'm thinking I'm really in it. The Feds on one side, Diamond Brain on the other. Couldn't get any worse, right?

Sure it could. A couple of days later I see Johnson waiting outside my apartment. "We're putting a man in with you," he said. "He's going to be on your wiring crew. We need you to cover for him. He's going to try and get Harding out. When the time comes—"

"I don't see Dr. Harding hardly at all." This was a lie. I met with her three or four afternoons a week, usually just half an hour or so. But I had her coming in my entrance, the one to the sub dock. Feds didn't know that one and I wanted to keep it that way.

Johnson skimmed right over it. "Well then, having an extra agent in there will help both of you. His name is Isaacson. You can vouch for him to your boss and he'll take it from there."

The Push was already making my head throb—betrayal, any betrayal, triggered the reaction— but I kept telling myself THEY WANT HARDING NOT BRAIN, and that kept me from stroking out on the spot. I didn't say anything more, just nodded.

In fairness, Isaacson wasn't that hard to deal with. Brain always let me take care of crew for the tech stuff, he didn't want to be bothered with details like that and he figured the Push was all the protection he needed. I pointed the kid at the dock conversion wiring we were doing below. That kept him out of my way and I figured that with so many people around, he couldn't cause that much trouble. My only concern was that he might see Amanda coming up to meet me but I solved that one by putting him on the reactor crew inside the sub we were hooking into the Rhodopsin Pulsar—that was what we were calling it; these villain guys, their stuff always had to have a cool name, and even Brain was a sucker for that.

Meanwhile me and Doc Harding were working out the Pulsar's frequency ranges and so on. The hell of it was, I genuinely liked her. We were getting to be friends. I was trying to keep my distance—I called her "doctor" even though she insisted I call her Amanda, and eventually we compromised on "Doc."

We were in my office, she was trying to explain how the neural impulses hit the brain, and then she paused for a minute and sighed. Out of nowhere she said, "I don't know, Ernie. Sometimes I get so excited about the possibilities. And then other times I wonder if we are doing the right thing. I mean, we're essentially trying to edit the human genome, aren't we? Isn't making people better the same rationale the Nazis used?"

I'd heard this argument before. "That's horseshit, doc. You been watching too many sci-fi movies about monsters. If you really believed that, then you would never have gotten into it in the first place. Making people better—making their lives better—is the whole point. Doctor Frankenstein is made up, he's fiction. Jonas Salk is real. My wife would be dead already without scientific advances. Hell, you wear glasses. You know what they called people with bad eyesight in primitive times?"

"Cursed?"

"They called 'em food." I grinned. "Me, I'm totally okay with science, especially when it keeps you from getting eaten. By dinosaurs or by cancer." I was trying to make a joke but it fell flat. I hadn't meant to bring up Debbie, it just kinda came out and my voice went a little bleak at the end.

"I didn't know you were married, Ernie." She laid a hand on mine. "I'm so sorry to hear about your wife being sick."

I shrugged. "She's hanging in there. We got her a private room at Resthaven. I see her as much as I can."

"But it's not looking good." It wasn't a question.

I just nodded.

She sat up. "Do you think the work we are doing here… possibly…?"

I scowled. I hadn't thought of that angle at all. "What, targeting—like, maybe—immune-response receptors? Something… I dunno, Doc, I never went to college. That's more your line. I just build stuff. But it's her white cell counts, not her brain. How could—"

"It's all connected." Doc Harding was getting excited; her earlier doubts were all gone now. "My initial breakthrough was with irradiated dihymenidrol. That compound, or something very like it, was the basis of the original Liberty Formula. I'm absolutely convinced of it. The right combination of radiation with a biochemical compound is the holy grail everyone's been chasing since… well, since the supers first appeared. We've all been obsessed with the biochemistry but what if the *radiation* is the key? A way to—I don't know—somehow electrically communicate through the pulse with the cells *themselves?* Not just influence neural impulses, but actually change DNA?"

I was keeping up, but just barely. "What, you mean fiddle this thing to tell Debbie's white cells to just… get better?"

"To stimulate healing. It's not as crazy as it sounds, Ernie. We use other devices for optimizing the body's healing abilities. Sterile environments, hyperbaric chambers. A lot of medicine is just about clearing the way for the human organism to cure itself." Her eyes were shining. "We could cure cancer. Regrow missing limbs for the crippled soldiers coming home from Vietnam. We could—"

"Whoa there, Doc, we got hired to do a specific job. I love your idea and God knows the world needs it, but Br—the boss is paying for all this, you think he'll go for it?"

"Of course he will. I'm his doctor. This effort is part of his therapy, that's why he brought me in. Finding a broader application could even help with the financing… though Ronald seems to have plenty of money."

I started to say, *And Brain's giant version you don't know about, that I got my guys working on down below? What part of the therapy is that?* But my head throbbed with a sharp warning pain and I couldn't get the words out. The Push was still working. Even so, I knew one thing now—there was no goddam way I was letting the Feds take Doc Harding while there was a chance she could save Debbie. I had to stall them—and Brain— at least until we got these new revisions to the prototype Pulsar working.

Somehow.

●●●

That was around the end of March. Two weeks later, it all went to hell.

It was Easter Sunday. I'd gone down to the warehouse lair because… well, because Debbie had been having a bad morning and we finally had to give her one of them pills the Resthaven docs had prescribed for pain and it just knocked her flat. I was just sitting and watching her sleep and thinking about how she used to love helping with the Easter Egg hunt our church did for the Sunday School kids.

What? Hell yeah, I went to church. I was a crook but I wasn't no heathen. And Debbie really felt strongly about it, so we went. It's what you do when you're married. She does your stuff, you do her stuff. Someday you'll know.

Anyway, sitting there looking at her, I was gonna start crying if I didn't get out and do something. So I thought screw it, I might as well work.

Sunday I should have had the place mostly to myself; it was a holiday, after all, and we were a working business, even if the business was crime. Normally there'd be just a couple of Brain's guards to keep out dockside riffraff, or send a warning if any cops showed up looking interested in the building. I waved at 'em when I come up through the dockside tunnel and they sorta grinned and saluted. Most of our crew were pretty good guys, really, it wasn't all evil sneers and shit like you see in the movies. We was just working stiffs when you scraped the paint off.

One of 'em, I think his name was Billy, nods at me and says, "Lady doc's in your office. And Brain is coming by later, he said yesterday he wanted to talk to you."

Well, that wasn't good. Brain, I mean. I figured Doc Harding just had a brain wave or something, or maybe she had a hard time with holidays too. But Brain might have figured out that we weren't really building what he asked for; the big one was going along okay, but the little one, the prototype Doc Harding called the Healing Ray, was a totally different thing than the Rhodopsin Pulsar. I had to figure out some kind of a stall to placate Brain that still counted as progress, a soft betrayal that wouldn't trigger the Push. So I was kinda distracted when I walked in and it took me a second to see what the lady doc was doing.

She wasn't looking at our test rats in the cage or staring at the blackboard like usual. Instead, she was sitting at our shared desk surrounded by piles of paper— invoices, bills of lading, materials requests. She looked up at me and said, "Ernie. What is Ronald building down below?"

"Didn't he tell you?" Tiny throb in my temples from the Push. *The doc's on our side, her knowing's not a betrayal.* I was getting good at damping it down but it was there.

"I think there are a great many things Ronald isn't telling me." Her voice was icy cold. "Like how his business is a cover for… I think the papers call him Diamond Brain?" She shook her head. "I'm such a fool. Dihymenidrol. Diamond. Dynamo. Under my nose all this time. Both him and Justin. I was so focused on my work—and *you!* With your condescending lecture about science and the good of humanity!"

The pain in my head was getting worse. *Divert. Change the subject.* "That was all true. I just come from Debbie's bedside for Chrissake. Settle down."

"First you tell me what those men are building down below. Ronald told me it was naval salvage, disassembling a submarine. But it's not. It's a giant rhodopsin flasher, isn't it? Using sonics you designed?"

I could only manage a nod.

"What is he planning, for God's sake?" I couldn't answer but she didn't notice. "At that size he could reach everyone in St. Jacques City. He's—oh, Jesus. He's not trying for a cure. He's trying for an *amplifier.* He's going to control every mind in the city. The gender block probably will be gone too. Ernie, why? What does he want?"

I said thickly, "He wants *you.* Can't you see it?"

She had her mouth open to say something but that stopped her. Finally she stuttered, "But… oh, my God. Ernie… that's impossible. He's… I'm—Damn it, I'm living with someone. I'm—oh, goddammit, Ernie, I like *women*, do you understand?"

And suddenly I did. Of course Brain knew she was a lez. That's why he was trying to get powered up. So he could Push her. Make her love him. Controlling St. Jacques City, that was just a bonus. "Now you like chicks, yeah. Later you won't. Not after he turns that thing on."

It took her a second, then she got it. Her face colored. Maybe embarrassed, maybe angry. "I have to talk to him. Make him see. This is… this is all wrong. Oh, Ernie. How could you…?"

"Please. Doc. Amanda. I'm begging you. I won't get in your way—" That last part gave me a quick pain spike. I ignored it. "—but help me save Debbie first. Please. We are so close—look at the samples from the rats—another couple of days, a week, tops."

"Sorry, Voskovec. Time's up for the doctor. You too."

This was a new voice. We both whipped around to see the Isaacson kid standing at the door. Holding a gun pointed at us.

He grinned at me. Hard grin, not with any humor in it. More like a tiger who's about to chow down on a nice juicy gazelle. "You thought your runaround was working on me, didn't you, Voskovec? I figured if I followed

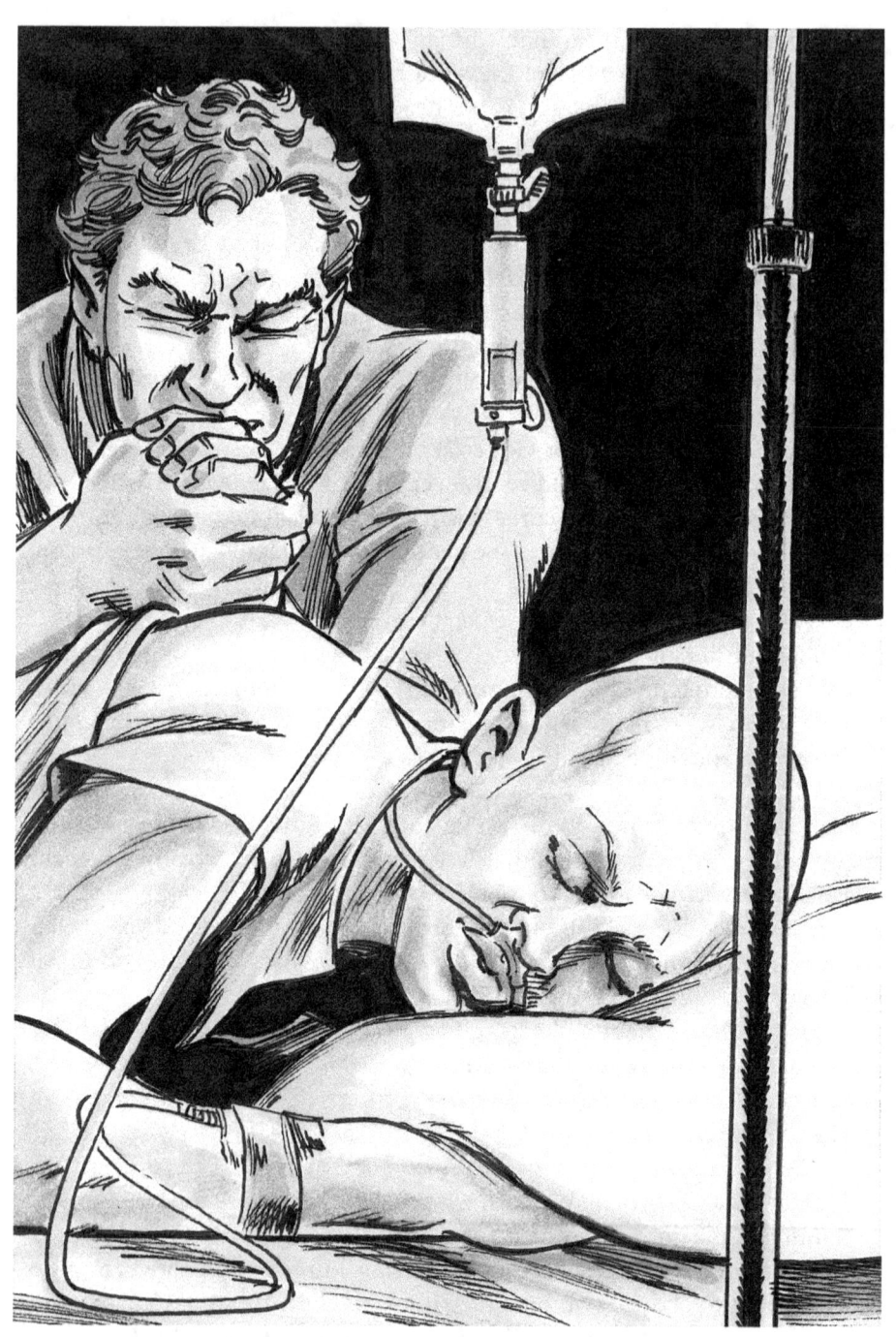

"…looking at her, I was going to start crying…"

you I'd find the doctor and here she is. You're both coming with me. Now. Cap Dynamo and a squad of cops are on their way and we need to get you folks out before they get here. Lot of folks waiting to talk to you, Harding. And probably Voskovec here too if he's been helping you."

There was no point in reminding him we had a deal. Even if he'd meant to honor the promises Johnson made me, and it didn't look like he did, he couldn't save Debbie. But the Healing Ray might.

The Push was buzzing in my head to *stop him, take him out, protect Brain*, and that fired my adrenaline. I nodded at the Doc, trying to put across the idea that she needed to distract him.

She got it right away. I told you she was a smart cookie. "You don't understand," she told Isaacson. "Whatever claim you think you have on me, you need to know that Ronald—the man you call Diamond Brain—he has a weapon that threatens all of—"

"No he doesn't," the kid cut in. "Jesus, how stupid d'you think I am? I planted explosives in the control center, I got the remote trigger right here." He reached into his pocket with his free hand and pulled out a little radio sender.

I was trying to think of something I could use as a weapon. My tool belt had a hammer and a couple of big wrenches—but it was on the desk and there was no way I could get to it before he shot me. I'd been inching back towards the wall, one hand behind my back, feeling for something I maybe could throw at him. But his words stopped me. The self-righteous little ass didn't understand what he'd done, but I did, and the realization shriveled my balls into twin nuggets of ice. "Where? Where's the bomb?"

"What does it matter?" Isaacson laughed.

"It matters because there's a goddamn *nuclear reactor* up there, you idiot," I snapped. "If your bomb blows the cooling system or the control rods, there's heavy water going everywhere, maybe a meltdown—Jesus Christ, how do you not *know* this? You've been working next to it for two weeks! You ignorant little—"

He glared at me and for a second I thought he might shoot me dead right then and there. Instead he took a deep breath and gestured with the gun. "All right. First we're going to take the doctor out to my van and cuff her and then you're going to show me how to—*aagh!*"

I hadn't found a weapon, but Doc Harding had. While he was focused on me she'd unclipped the fire extinguisher on the wall, and suddenly she swung it up and brought it down on his head, hard. There was an ugly wet crunch and he collapsed to the floor. Blood was coming out his ears.

"Did I… oh, God, did I kill him?'"" Doc Harding looked like she might throw up.

"Probably. That doesn't matter. Right now we gotta—oh, Jesus." The radio sender had rolled out of his hand and I saw a red light on it was blinking. His hand might have spasmed, or he might have fallen on it. Whatever. The trigger had been pulled.

I coulda built that thing smaller, I thought, crazily. Weird what goes through your head at times like that.

Then came the sound of an explosion.

We ran out of the office to the catwalk that gave us a view of the whole underground dock. I looked up to where the control center was.

"Shit!" It was as bad as I thought. The coolant pipes were shattered and spraying water everywhere, and it looked like there was sparks coming out of the control arrays too.

I don't know if I'm putting this across, what a Christless mess that kid Isaacson had made of everything. See, the warehouse was basically a shell over a squared-off pit that was originally going to be the submarine dock. We hadn't really changed any of that, and there was even still a pool with open water from the bay at the bottom, with offices surrounding it along the wall, and stairways and catwalks strung every which way. A lot of it was fragile, improvised stuff, because it was still under construction. The reactor core was at the center of all this, in a control shack that hung suspended over the pool. We had pillars and rebar set up as supports but the concrete hadn't been poured yet, because we'd never have gotten the reactor in there afterward, it was too big.

Understand? We were still doing the rebuild on the place, we hadn't put in new walls or reinforced concrete or anything like that, not around the reactor. That was slated for the next week, but it was too late. Right then it was still an old dockside warehouse, mostly two-by-fours and exposed wiring. It would never have passed a legit safety inspection, but we weren't a legit operation.

Bottom line? Those sparks would have the whole building blazing in no time. I could already see some of the steps leading up there starting to catch fire.

Doc Harding was clutching my arm, her face white with horror. I shook her off. "Doc, I gotta get up there, get the rods in all the way, try and keep the whole place from going. Grab the prototype ray and get out—"

Shouts were coming from all over and then I heard Brain yelling my name. "Voskovec! *Voskovec!* What is all this?"

"It's your death knell, you murderer!" The topside door to the outer office facade blew off its hinges and there was Cap Dynamo in his glittering blue-and-gold outfit. He jumped, an impossible leap that took him in a long arc, almost the length of the whole sub dock, to land on the catwalk a few feet from where Brain was standing. "Give it up, you—"

Brain didn't let him finish, but pulled some kind of gun—not standard, I think it was the multi-level laser blaster I'd built for him a while back—and red light lanced out at Cap Dynamo. It should have cut him in half but he was wearing some kind of refractive armor under that blue and gold, or maybe it was his own innate invulnerability. The blast staggered him but that was all. It didn't stop him. The two men closed in a fighting clinch.

"Justin!" Doc Harding screamed. "Ronald! Both of you! Stop this, can't you see—"

"They can't hear you!" I grabbed her and shook her. "It doesn't *matter*, we're all going up in radioactive flames if we don't get the reactor tamped down! Goddammit, listen to me!"

But she was beyond any persuasion by then. I don't think she heard me at all. She twisted away. "All of this—my fault—all my fault—" She ran toward the stairs. "I have to stop them!"

I looked up and saw the fire was spreading. There were more shouts and I heard shooting. Apparently Cap Dynamo had brought cops with him. We only had a skeleton crew but they were putting up a fight, sounded like.

Isaacson was dead and the Doc was out of it. No one knew about the reactor but me. I heard a crash and saw the stairs to the control center collapse in a shower of fire and sparks.

Shit. Now what? I had the Push in my head, prodding me forward. *Save Brain. Save the reactor. Save everything.* That and desperation got me moving. The stairs were gone but I remembered a ladderway on the opposite wall. That would take me part way up.

There wasn't any rope or anything like that but we had spools of insulated wire we hadn't used yet. I could improvise something, maybe reach the rafters and come at it from above. If the control rods were intact. If I didn't get my ass shot off in the crossfire between the cops and our guys. If I didn't fall and break my fool neck. If. If. If.

Screw it. I grabbed my tool belt from the desk and moved.

The battle was getting closer; I could hear it up top. The cops were forcing our guys back. I ran around the edge of the pool to the opposite wall, sure that any second a stray bullet was going to drill me in the back. I'd lost track of Doc Harding, but Brain and Cap Dynamo were bouncing all over the catwalks, throwing punches and yelling at each other. But I didn't dare pay attention. The Push was throbbing in my head like a migraine, except it wasn't pain now, it was compulsion. *Save Brain. Save everything.* I stopped at one of the big wire spools and used my nippers to cut myself a big coil of rubberized wire, then I got to the ladder and took the rungs two at a time, the tool belt thumping awkwardly on my hips.

At the top of the ladder I stopped. I was maybe ten feet above and thirty feet away from where the control shack with the reactor was sitting, the pillars with the wooden slats and the rebar—all ready for a concrete pour the next morning— frustratingly out of reach. If I tried to jump I'd just bounce down to the pool and fracture my skull, or maybe impale myself on a length of rebar. No place to climb to it.

You're an engineer, degree or no degree. Work the problem.

Okay, can't jump, can't climb. That left what? My brain, buzzing with the Push, was working faster than it ever had. I'd cut the wire thinking vaguely I could use it as a climbing rope, but there was nothing to tie it to. The rubberized length of wiring was too stiff and heavy to try and lasso the rebar or anything crazy like that.

Work the problem, my brain kept telling me. Or maybe it was the Push.

Suddenly I saw how to do it. Rafters. We had open rafters still. And I had the wire, and my tool belt. It was nuts but it was my only shot. I had to try it or we were all dead. Me, Brain, the Doc, the crew and the cops, probably everyone around the bay if the reactor went critical.

Tottering awkwardly at the top of the ladder, I looped the end of the wire around the neck of my hammer, twisting and tying it so it would stay, just barely managing not to drop it... or fall. Normally there was no way I'd be physically capable of this kind of thing, but with the added adrenaline of the Push... I could feel it, like liquid fire in my veins. Upping my game. My body felt hot and loose and limber. *Save Brain. Save the reactor. Save everything.*

I shifted so I was hanging on to the ladder with one hand and with the other I swung the wire, weighted with the hammer, up toward the rafters. It was too stiff to wrap around but I didn't need it to. It sailed up and over and I fed out more slack till the end with the hammer was almost level with me. I almost ran out of wire but thankfully I'd cut enough of it that I could grip one end in each hand. Carefully, I untangled my hammer and put it back in my belt, gripping the ends of the wire in my teeth—I was having the hell of a time hanging on, especially trying to get the hammer loose one-handed, but I didn't want it in my way and I thought I might need it later. But finally

I was ready. I had one end of the wire in each hand. I looked up and said a little prayer and jumped.

I swung up and out, missing the roof of the control shack by inches, trying not to think about the flames climbing up the wall, or if the rafter the wire was looped around could take my weight. Thankfully the rubber insulation kept the wire from slipping through my hands, though I could feel it cutting into my fingers. Well, not really, but it felt like it was.

I swung back toward the wall and kicked out again toward where the control center hung. This one was better, my body arcing almost gracefully up over the roof of the shack. I let go at the top of the arc and that was it for graceful. I fell onto the aluminum roof and felt it buckle. One of the slats came completely loose and I tumbled through to the floor of the shack, the edge of the slat tearing at my face and arm. I could feel it ripping my shirt and probably my arm, but there was no time to think about that.

Inside the shack the computers were largely intact. But the dials were all redlining. No coolant; half the water that was supposed to serve that purpose was spraying all over to hell and gone from the broken pipes, some of it turning to superheated steam. Goddam it, how was I the only one that knew we had a reactor going critical? Couldn't Brain see this mess up here?

I don't know if you've ever seen a sub reactor. This one was fairly compact— had to be, it was meant to be aboard a ship at sea. A metal sphere maybe five feet in diameter with control rods coming out the top kind of like the leaves on a pineapple. But vertical. Twenty-four of them. Most of them were about halfway up and they all needed to be pushed down as far as they would go… but first I needed to deal with the coolant problem.

Naval equipment has multiple redundancies. Ship at sea, remember. So there were multiple water intakes. We were just piping the stuff up from the bay, using the pool down below. The question was whether or not that asshole Issacson had blown all of the intake pipes or if there were any left intact. If there were, I could close the valves on the bad ones and with the rods all the way down, the pipes that were still working could get pressure up again, assuming everything could take the load.

So first order of business was figuring out if I had working pipes at all. I could hear water hissing so something was getting in there. Which ones? I leaned out the door and nearly slipped and fell on something slick.

Blood. Mine. I looked down and saw my arm was all torn up under my shredded sleeve, a little parting gift from the fall through the aluminum roof. I hardly felt it. The Push was vibrating through my whole body with rage and urgency.

All right, Doctor Fixit, let's see what you've really got. I looked around the warehouse, ignoring the fire and the gunshots and the screams coming from every direction, and concentrated on the pipes coming up from below. Fortunately I knew which was which; I'd designed the damn thing. The ones on the west wall were blown and venting water and steam everywhere. But the ones on the east wall were okay. So… intakes One and Three needed the valves closed.

Too hot to do it barehanded, of course. The whole room was sweltering from the fire and the reactor. My shirt was a lost cause anyway. I tore it off and ripped it in half, wrapping my hands and spinning the wheels of first One and then Three. Done.

Now the rods. One at a time, steady pressure, don't shove or they'll jam up. The heat was abating a little, I thought, though it might have been my imagination. I glanced over at the dials and saw the needles were slowly dropping below redline.

"Sonofabitch," I muttered. "It worked. Praise Jesus." I had nineteen of the twenty-four down flush with the surface of the sphere and I was almost limp with relief.

Then it all went to hell again. There was a huge crash and the floor lurched under me. The reactor was bolted to the floor on four sides; but it didn't hold. Two of the four legs tore loose. I slid toward the wall and almost out the open door to the catwalk, but there wasn't a catwalk, not any more.

Cap Dynamo and Brain fell through the torn roof. Brain had the blaster in one hand and Cap had him by the wrist, holding the gun away from him. They were still trading punches with their free hands. Any one of those punches would have taken my head off, but they were both supers. I could see bruises forming and healing on both of their faces with inhuman speed. It was fascinating and horrifying and for a second I was hypnotized by the sheer alien weirdness of it. These guys—they weren't really human. Not any more.

"Stop!" My voice was hoarse and cracking. "Jesus Christ, you guys! Brain! The reactor—you idiots are—"

Brain saw me and his face twisted with rage. "Voskovec! I should have known—you stinking Judas…"

Judas. *The betrayer.*

My synapses flared with involuntary conditioning as the Push kicked in. Searing pain exploded in my skull. Suddenly my legs didn't work and my arms were as loose as a marionette's with the strings cut. Red mist floated over my eyes.

Cap Dynamo was still struggling with Brain's gun arm. The blaster wobbled and a red beam lanced up and out through the roof, slicing through one of the supports. The shack jerked again.

Then came a scream. "Ronald, Justin, stop! Please!" Doc Harding was standing on the torn catwalk. There was maybe a seven-yard gap between the dangling end of the catwalk and the door of the control shack. She was waving frantically with one hand and hanging on for dear life with the other. "For the love of God, *end* this! Neither one of you can win!"

It surprised Brain long enough that Cap Dynamo was able, at last, to wrench Brain's arm down and away—but the blaster was still firing. The red beam swung down and around and sliced Amanda Harding neatly in half, diagonally, from the right collarbone down to her left hip. Her mouth made a soft round O of shock and then she was dead, just two cauterized hunks of meat falling to the pool below.

Cap Dynamo let out a roar of rage and pain and almost in one motion, spun Brain around like a rag doll and twisted his head between his hands. Even over the crackle of the fire and the gunshots, I heard Brain's neck snap. The Push in my head died with him. I could feel it.

But I still couldn't feel my legs and I knew I never would again. The floor lurched again and then we were falling. *All for nothing,* I thought bitterly. *Debbie's dead now and so am I. I killed myself for nothing.*

I waited to feel the impact that would end everything for good but I never did. I passed out before we hit bottom.

●●●

I opened my eyes and everything was white.

At first I honest to God thought it was the afterlife. Then I blinked and I saw it was just white drapes. It was a hospital room. "Where—?"

"Bayview Medical," a voice said. "Just out of intensive care. I'm glad you're finally awake, Mr. Voskovec."

It was Cap Dynamo. He was sitting at the foot of the bed, a newspaper folded over his lap. It was weird how normal he looked, considering the mask and the blue-and-gold spandex outfit he was wearing.

"You got me out?" I asked him.

"Mostly a matter of shifting wreckage out of the way and keeping your head above water while I did it. Miraculously, you didn't break any bones." He smiled ruefully at me. "Even at that, I wasn't sure you were going to make it."

"Me neither," I croaked. "What happened with the reactor?"

"It's still underwater, at the bottom of the submarine dock in what's left of the warehouse. The whole waterfront is cordoned off and a Navy crew is working on disposal now. I gather from what the nuclear specialists tell me that your quick thinking bought us the time we needed and saved a lot of lives, including mine. Even with my advantages I don't think I could survive a nuclear meltdown." He smiled. "You can relax. There will be no criminal charges. However you got embroiled with the Brain, we owe you a debt of gratitude. You're a hero."

"Go to hell, you bastard. I'm no freakin' hero, *Justin*."

That straightened him up. "Excuse me?"

"You heard me. Screw you and your hero shit. That might be good enough for the papers but here it's just you and me and we know better. Amanda Harding is dead and that's on you."

He didn't say anything but from his eyes I knew I'd scored a hit. His broad shoulders sagged and he wasn't Cap Dynamo any more, just a sad man in a silly leotard. "I know," he said, softly. "I never meant for her... for anyone..."

I wasn't having any. "Spare me your suffering bullshit nobility, hero. You didn't want anyone to get *hurt*? Are you seriously going to try and sell that? You dress up in that fool outfit to go out and break heads. For whatever reason. Maybe it gets you off. I don't effing care. You and your boys charged in there with no plan, no nothing, just to break shit and hit people. Well, guess what? Blowing up complex equipment is *dangerous*. You could have done it without setting the entire goddam block on fire. You had a guy inside who should have told you what was up. Instead *he planted explosives next to a nuclear reactor*. Why? For the glory? For the rush? For *fun?*"

He was silent.

"Here's something else for you to suffer over, Justin. We were maybe three days away from curing cancer. Me and Doc Harding almost had it cracked. But the prototype ray's destroyed with the rest of the wreckage and even if it wasn't, she was the key to getting it working. The Doc was the only one that understood the relationship between the radiation and the biochemistry. Now she's dead. Thanks to you."

Still nothing.

I exploded, "Jesus! What does it take to get through to you? D'you even know what you *did*? What your government buddies did? All of you, you're worse than Brain! At least he was an honest crook! He just wanted to be rich and get laid! You assholes, you wrap it in the flag and act all freakin'

Cap Dynamo let out a roar of rage and pain...

noble but the bottom line is you just push everybody around same as Brain did!"

"That's not true. I thought… we thought… we had a duty. We thought we were helping." He stood. "I know that's hard for you to believe right now. But it's the truth."

I let it go. He wasn't getting it.

He paused at the door. "If there's anything I can do… you have a blank check."

I snorted. "Buying my silence?"

"Showing our gratitude."

When I didn't reply he sighed and turned to go.

"Wait."

He stopped but didn't turn around. "Yes?"

"My wife Debbie. She's at Resthaven. You cover the cost of her room there, her therapy, whatever treatments she needs, all of it. For life. Yeah? Your blank check cover that?"

"Of course." His voice was stronger now that I'd given him a way to atone.

But I wasn't done. "And see if you can't think up a way to 'help' that doesn't involve hitting people and breaking shit. You can do incredible things. Maybe find how to use that to serve people without dressing in a stupid leotard and being a bullying jock asshole about it."

He didn't answer, but his shoulders slumped again. And then he was gone.

●●●

"And that was the last anyone saw of Cap Dynamo. I guess he took what I said to heart. He got off easy, though." Voskovec's voice was bleak and bitter. "I found out after he left that Debbie was already dead. She passed some time Sunday night or early Monday morning. Never even woke up from that last pain pill."

Christine didn't know what to reply to that. She finally said, softly, "I'm so sorry, Mr. Voskovec."

"It's okay, kid. In a way it was a blessing. She never knew about me and the supers. And she knew she was loved. I made sure of that." He grinned. "The éclair place, they're still in business, you know. Resthaven's gone now but the bakery's hanging in there. Just like me."

Christine nodded and shut off the tape recorder. "I think that's a good place to end this, Mr. Voskovec." She stood up.

"Call me Ernie, kid. And come by again sometime. I'd like to hear how you're doing."

"I will." She paused. "Cap was right, you know. You were a hero."

"Pardon my French, kid, but eff that." Voskovec snorted. "This hero-villain shit, it's kid's games. Most people, they're just people. Even us guys that were henching it back then. Put *that* in your story."

Christine nodded and left.

She stopped at the front desk to sign out. A tall man with silver hair and broad shoulders was at the desk. The girl was saying, "He's got someone with him, but I'm sure—oh, here she is now. So he's free if you want to go in."

"He won't want to see me. I'm just checking on his condition." The voice was deep, sonorous, and somehow a little sad. He nodded at Christine and Christine nodded back and headed for the exit.

"If you say so." The girl at the desk was still talking. "In that case, is there anything else we can do for the Harding Foundation today? You are our major supporter here; we can at least get you a coffee."

"No, that's fine. I wanted a word with the floor nurse but otherwise there's nothing that can't wait for the monthly board meeting."

Christine paused at the door. There was something about the tall man… then she realized what she'd heard.

Harding?

Could it be coincidence?

She turned and said "Cap?" And then added softly, "…Justin?"

The tall man stiffened. For barely a second.

But he didn't answer, just went on down the corridor to the nurse's station. Christine thought of chasing him, but let it go.

Like Ernie said. People were just people, after all.

THE END

FIGHTING THE ADAM WEST FIGHT

In its original incarnation, this was my contribution to a superhero anthology project that ended up stillborn. The call was for stories showing the darker, edgier side of superheroes, and to attempt to look at the pulp-hero genre in new ways.

Now, I have to confess, as much as I love Batman and the Shadow and the Spider, I tend to cringe a little when I hear editors talking about getting dark and edgy with superheroes. It happened in comics with *Watchmen* and it happened in movies with *The Dark Knight*— people get so excited about seeing something done in this new way that they think everything could be done in this new way. Not everything can. And when it's done badly, you are left with the impression of a petulant nerd writer still trying to prove that it's okay to like superhero comics to all the jocks that are jeering at him for it.

"He's still fighting the Adam West fight," is how my friends and I refer to it. You can always tell when someone's fighting the Adam West fight in a modern superhero story; mostly because there will be jarringly inappropriate sex scenes, the violence is way over the top, and everyone swears like a sailor— but it's still your basic *chase, explosion, good guy hits bad guy, the end* plot.

I did my time fighting the Adam West fight, and at first I was thinking this project didn't sound like something I'd have anything to add to. But then I noticed that the previously published work set in the same super-hero universe we were to use, our source material, leapfrogged from the forties to the modern day. Very little had been written in the novels or the submissions guide about what was going on in "St. Jacques City" in the sixties.

Well, hell, that was my wheelhouse. 1967 to 1980 or thereabouts: Batman, Bond, and bionics. Those were *my* superpeople. I'm familiar with the pulp heroes of the thirties and forties, but they aren't baked into my DNA the way the late sixties/early seventies heroes are. Why not do the Adam West fight for real? *Let's take that era and put a new-pulp spin on it,* I thought.

This came together in my head with another story idea I'd been playing with off and on for years... Who built the Batcave? Who hollowed out the volcano for SPECTRE's underground headquarters in *You Only Live Twice?* I mean, those are huge, HUGE undertakings. Here in Seattle they've been trying to dig a tunnel that will take Highway 99 underground for about twelve blocks and that's taken over four years and gone millions over budget. Granted, there were no evil super-geniuses on board the 99 tunnel project to speed up its efficiency, but even so... that shit is hard to pull off. How do bad guys do it? Who's their contractor?

Ernie Voskovec, handyman to the supervillains, is my answer to that question.

Those two ideas came together and then the thing practically wrote itself.

I also tried to play with the idea that everyone thinks they're a good guy, even when they are clearly bad people doing bad things. Plus, per the editorial instruction, there is violence and sexuality, even if it's a bit toned down from the usual grim-n-gritty super stuff that saw print throughout the 1990s. That seemed edgy and dark enough for St. Jacques City... and I tried to make it genuinely adult as opposed to the usual arrested-adolescent take you get when superhero writers are trying to prove how grown-up they can be.

It was tremendous fun to tell this story, mostly because I kept seeing it as a movie in my head. Rather arrogantly, I even mentally cast it with actors who were current in the story's setting, the superhero/sci-fi milieu of the groovy sixties and bionic seventies. Ernie Voskovec is, of course, Ernest Borgnine from around the time of *The Poseidon Adventure.* Cap Dynamo is somewhere between early 70s Gary Collins and late 60s Frank Converse. Amanda Harding is Diana Muldaur from the time she was on *McCloud.* And Diamond Brain is Tony Perkins from somewhere in the mid-70s when he was working on things like *ffolkes* and *The Black Hole.* So as you read it, feel free to picture those people in the roles... and the soundtrack is that groovy bass-and-bongos action jazz stuff you got back then, too; I had that going in the background all the time I was writing. The rhodopsin flasher is a concept I lifted from Alfred Bester's *The Demolished Man,* one of the great science fiction novels of all time, since I was thinking of this as a sort of Alfred Bester joint anyway... though his use of the concept is nothing like mine, nevertheless it's a sort of homage to his style of SF, where the action gets really wild and crazy but everything is technically correct.

So there you go. The story behind the story. Hope you enjoyed it, along with this little peek into the process.

●●●

PIMPIN' YOUR SUPERCAR
A DR. FIXIT TALE
By Greg Hatcher

Christine Vance glared at the floor nurse. "But he *knows* me. I've been here before."

"Doesn't matter." The nurse was stolid and expressionless, a thickly-built woman in her mid-fifties. She looked as immovable as Gibraltar. "Mr. Voskovec was very specific. No room for doubt. No visitors." She tapped a red laminated sign hanging from the doorknob to Ernie Voskovec's room with the words PRIVACY PROTOCOL printed on it in black letters.

Christine noticed the door was ajar. She leaned to the side and raised her voice. "Ernie! It's Christine! Are you up and around?" The floor nurse glared and opened her mouth to speak but before any words came out Christine added, "I brought doughnuts!"

"Doughnuts? Hot damn." The door swung open and there was Ernie Voskovec beaming at her from his wheelchair. He looked up at the nurse and said in an apologetic tone, "I'm sorry, Flo. I shoulda given you a list of okay folks. I just never get real visitors, usually, and I didn't want any reporters." His eyes twinkled and his seamed walnut-brown face split in a big smile. "Also? Anybody with pastry, you send 'em straight in. Even that asshole Gerry Baylor from the *Star*." The nurse nodded and moved to make a note on her clipboard and Voskovec paled. "No, I'm kidding, never let Baylor in here, I don't care if he's got prime rib." He turned to face Christine and added ruefully, "Him and that other guy, whatshisface, Heston over at *Newstime*, they're the reason I asked 'em to put the sign up. Those guys are getting on my last goddamn nerve. Anyway, c'mon in, toots." He pivoted his wheelchair with surprisingly easy grace, adding over his shoulder to the nurse, "You can put Chrissy here on the good list though, no press guys is what I meant. She's okay."

"Already done."

"Thanks." Voskovec turned back toward the room and wheeled himself in.

The nurse glanced at Christine, still expressionless, but somehow no longer hostile. "Vance? V-A-N-C-E?"

"Yes ma'am." Christine smiled brilliantly at her, trying to keep the gloat out of it. *No need to antagonize her; if Ernie agrees to my proposal I'll be spending a lot of time here.* She stepped into the room.

Ernie was over by the window, gazing out over the rest home's court-yard. He looked a little annoyed and Christine was apprehensive. "What are you looking at, Ernie?"

"Saw somebody out by the hedge. You being here made me wonder if Baylor was going to take another swing at it but it's just that idiot Merkel who's over in the other wing across from mine." At her blank expression he added, "He's trying to sneak a smoke. I don't know how he gets 'em in over there, they're all on staff watch, that's what 'skilled nursing' means. It's code for 'can't be trusted alone.' They get pretty strict here about stuff like that, the whole place went nonsmoking a couple months ago." He sighed. "I don't care about that but man, I miss having a cold beer in the afternoon. They don't let us have nothing. Flo was giving you the stinkeye and all you brought was doughnuts. That's practically contraband here." Abruptly Voskovec wheeled around to face her as though making a deliberate effort to shake off his pensive mood. He grinned. "Where are they, anyway? Give."

Christine smiled, relieved to see him in good spirits again. She handed him a small white bag. "I didn't know what you like so I brought an assortment." She paused. "I'm press too, you know, Ernie."

"I know. National Radio or whatever—"

"National Public Radio. NPR."

"Yeah, that." Ernie raised a roguish eyebrow. "But you're easy on the eyes, kid. Baylor's got a face like an overcooked potato and a voice only another foghorn could love. Sweet young thing like you, though…" Christine flushed and Ernie's grin softened. "Naw, I'm just funning with you, toots. You blush so easy; it makes it hard not to tease you a little." He grew serious. "No, really, I was just happy to see you so I could say thanks. I listened to that thing you did about me and Justin. You didn't use our names. You could have. I mean, I knew you was taping, I know how radio works."

"I just… it wasn't that kind of story." She shook her head. "The story was what really happened back then with Captain Dynamo and Diamond Brain and the battle of Easter Sunday, and that's where I tried to keep it. People want to know about the old St. Jacques supers and what that life was like. Masks and costumes and battles on the streets and all of that. So that's what I gave them. Anyway, you're a source," she finished. "I don't reveal sources. I'm kind of surprised anyone found you at all. I didn't even tell my boss who Dr. Fixit was. I don't know how the *Star* or *Newstime* got hold of it."

"I know it wasn't you. You'd have done it on the radio already if you was gonna do it. Naw, I think it was one of the night guys here, recognized my voice from the piece you did and tried to peddle it to somebody. Probably that punk that does such a shitty job mopping, that's got the headphones on all the time." He shrugged. "Doesn't matter. I don't talk to them reporters, they can't do nothing. Everybody else who knew the real story is dead— other'n you and me. I just get sick of them bugging me about it." He grinned at her and raised his eyebrow again, this time with a wry expression. "But that journalist source stuff ain't why you did it. You didn't just find me, you found Captain goddamn *Dynamo*. That's Pulitzer territory, you know it is. They been after him for years, folks saying he was dead or gone back to his home planet or whatever the hell nutcase theory of the week. You didn't give him up either. Your boss must've chewed your ass good." Suddenly he paused, realizing. "Hey, that why you're here today? To warn me it's getting out? I know it can't be just bringin' an old man doughnuts."

"No, your privacy is still intact. Certainly as far as NPR is concerned. I admit that my producer and I discussed it. It was…" Now it was Christine who had a wry smile. "…well, it was spirited. But I finally persuaded him that both you and Justin had found… I don't know. A kind of accommodation. Peace, even. And that we shouldn't ruin that for the sake of a story. Of course I was tempted by the thought of going public with Justin being Captain Dynamo, but…." She shrugged helplessly. "Honestly? I don't know why I backed off, exactly. I think I felt a little sorry for him. Remember what you told me about people the last time I was here?"

"What? That folks are just folks what really only want to live their lives? Even the supers?"

Christine nodded.

Voskovec chuckled. "I knew you must'a liked that one because you put it in the radio thing. Well, anyway, I figure I owe you something, kid, and not just for the doughnuts. Although bless your heart for bringin' em." He opened the bag and whistled. "Damn, a maple bar. You must want something good." He pulled it out of the bag and admired it for a moment before taking a bite.

Christine was silent, letting him chew.

Voskovec finished the maple bar in moments and sighed with pleasure. Then he sat up a little and looked at Christine with his bright blue eyes. Christine had forgotten how powerful those eyes could be, clear and sharp and glittering with intelligence. They made him intimidating, even at his age and with him confined to a wheelchair.

Voskovec scowled, then grinned. "Okay then. So you don't want to give me up and you don't want to tell me some other reporter might do it. So what is it? What can Dr. Fixit do for you? Another radio story?"

"No. I'm not actually here for NPR today, this is for me." Christine hesitated. *Oh, hell, just tell him.* She took a deep breath and blurted, "I was hoping…. I thought maybe we could write a book."

"A book?" Ernie's eyebrows shot up. He looked genuinely surprised.

"I've been thinking about it ever since we did the original interview." Christine knew she was flushing again. She ignored it and plunged ahead, the words coming in a tumbling rush. "You're such a wonderful storyteller, and you operated as Dr. Fixit for… well, you said you started in 1956, right? And the Battle of Easter Sunday was 1968. Twelve years. And not just with Diamond Brain. You said you worked with the Midnight Midas, Devilhound, Ocean Bandit, the Electric Ladyland Mob…. How many others?"

"Christ, I don't know. Practically all of them, I guess. Well, not Lizard King. That guy was a creep. Had a thing for underage… never mind. Nice girl like you don't need to hear about that. All I'm saying is, yeah, I was a crook but I had *standards.*" Voskovec shook his head. "You understand, I never was around for the costumes and fistfights and shit, though. Dr. Fixit was just what the villain guys called me; they were all so obsessed with giving everything a cool-sounding name. But it wasn't like I dressed up or wore a mask or nothing. I never made the papers. I just built stuff."

Christine had to laugh. "Ernie, you built *death rays.* And super vehicles and secret lairs and—God, I don't even know. But you were right there, in the thick of it. You must have stories."

Voskovec looked a little sheepish. "Well, yeah, I can't deny I saw some shit." His eyes drifted away from Christine, looking off into the distance. "You remember Ghostwalker?"

"Before my time. I'm twenty-two, Ernie."

Voskovec let out a brief, braying laugh. "Yeah, I guess so. You said super vehicles, it reminded me of the one hero job I ever did. Around 1962, I guess it woulda been. I know it was before the Beatles."

"A job for Ghostwalker?"

"Yeah." Now Voskovec was the one flushing. "I never told anybody this story, it woulda finished me in the business for sure, maybe even got me killed. But…" He let out a long sigh. " …I built the Ghostmobile."

Christine suppressed a giggle. *He said that like somebody admitting they worked in porn.* But she just said mildly, "Okay, *that's* got to be a story worth telling." She leaned forward and smiled. "I hope you understand, Ernie, it's not about me or my career or anything like that. I just think—there's a whole secret history here in St. Jacques City, one that people should know about. It's why I started researching the supers in the first place. And you know that history, Ernie, you lived it."

"Lived *through* it, more like." Voskovec made a sour face. "Even behind the scenes like I was, shit got scary sometimes. Ghostwalker—that was a hero job and it almost got me murdered. If you only knew..."

"But that's my point, Ernie." Christine looked at him and leaned forward. "I'd like to know. People *should* know."

Voskovec's brow furrowed. "Maybe," he said at last. "How are you thinking we'd do this?"

"We tape you again, to start. Not for the radio, just for me. Then I go home and write it up. You look at it and tell me any changes you think I should make. Rinse and repeat till we have a book." Christine added after a moment, "Strictly anonymous if that's how you want it. We can say it's *as-told-to*...well, whatever name you want to use."

"Don't you want your name on it either, kid?"

"I just want to do the book. I told you it's not about me. Of course I'd see to it you got paid."

Voskovec snorted, then smiled. "I know that, kid. You got a good heart. I trust you. It ain't that."

"Then what?"

He scowled and leaned back in the wheelchair. "Not sure, to be honest," he admitted. "Maybe... you keep saying people should know but maybe they don't *want* to know, see what I mean? Like the Ghostmobile job, it got pretty ugly toward the end."

"Tell me. You know by now I can take it." Christine smiled and pulled the tape recorder out of her purse. "In fact, let's just go ahead and roll tape and I'll write it up at home this week and then bring it back Saturday for you to say yes or no. It'll be our trial run. What do you say?"

"Hmm." Voskovec considered it. He hunkered down in his wheelchair, chin resting on one fist. His gaze drifted away from Christine into the remembering place, again. Then he sat up and nodded. "Sure. Let's try it. Most of these folks are gone now anyway. Even Ghostwalker's retired, finally. Anyway..." his teeth bared in the roguish grin again. "It really is the hell of a story. It happened like this..."

⊚⊙⊚

Okay, I know you researched all this so you know the supers started with the Liberty Formula back in '42, during the war. You had the nuclear guys down in New Mexico and you had the bio-lab guys up here at Fort Wheeler, it's a museum now but it used to be an actual army base. The Fort Wheeler guys hit on the serum that made Sergeant Smasher and Liberty Jane and the rest of the Liberty Brigade. I don't know what was in the books and clippings and so on you read, but the deal was they managed to create about, oh, somewhere between fifteen and twenty supers, I guess. Some of them went nuts; the formula did something to their brains, and one of them, called himself... I think it was Arclight, something like that. The electric guy. He decided what they was doing up at the lab there was against God or whatever and blew it all up in '44. Killed the scientist guys, burned the lab to the ground, then took himself out before the MPs even woke up enough to move in on him. And of course the Army covered it up, they didn't want Adolf's boys to know about the formula, that's why they put the Brigade in the masks and all in the first place. The idea was to sell the story that... okay, I see you nodding there. You know all this.

But the thing was, the Brigade, they stayed together after the war. Some of them did, anyway. It kind of got its own momentum going. It was Liberty Jane set the tone and the agenda, made it more about disaster rescue and citizen volunteer stuff like the Liberty Mission down there on Tenth—I think they're still on Tenth, I dunno, it's not like I get the newsletter.

And they fought crime. Street crime, mostly, they didn't have their act together enough to go after the serious mob guys. Though I think J. Edgar's boys might've tipped 'em on places they thought needed raiding but didn't have the evidence to get a warrant for it. Hoover had kind of a flexible relationship with due process sometimes, if you know what I'm sayin'.

So by the time I'm in the business, mid-fifties, Liberty Jane's retired, she's mostly running the foundation, the Brigade's a civilian thing. They had the headquarters up there on Lincoln Hill by the observatory.

And there were new members. The wartime folks are mostly gone by that point and now we're seeing this new breed, the science heroes. Remember them? Not supers, these were regular folks, but with tech that made 'em a match for any super. Ironmonger, Electric Eel, Jumping Jax, Firedancer. That crowd. They didn't get as much press as the wartime crew. Press didn't warm to 'em the way they did the Brigade. Though a lot of 'em were like, auditioning. The Brigade was still active. In fact they was supposed to be running point on the Bay of Pigs but Firedancer put the kibosh on that, she was half-Jamaican and she had a real bee in her bonnet about colonialist stuff, she liked Castro. She was one of the ones HUAC was looking at for a while there, but Hoover shut that down, he didn't want his pet supers dragged into no hearing.

Sergeant Smasher was still the leader; as late as 1960 he could still bench-press a trailer truck, and the first-generation supers didn't age as fast as regular folks. I'll tell you flat out, I can't prove it or nothing, but some of the guys used to talk about how the original wartime supers had faked dying and gone underground. Just to get away from the government trying to dissect them and get at the Liberty Formula, you know, recreate it somehow. Especially once a couple of bright Pentagon research guys realized it was possibly a way to immortality.

There were other rogue supers showing up too. Not Liberty Formula ones, either—radiation-based mutation gave us a couple. Cetacean, the fish guy, he was from the Bikini Islands where they did all that nuclear testing. Then there was the Indonesian kid, I forget his name but he could fly and he was a pyrokinetic too. He could point at a car or a warehouse or something and it'd just ignite. Not much control, though, and I don't think he lasted long. Warehouse explosion got him.

But sooner or later they all ended up here in St. Jacques City because the Brigade's here, see? So you'd get Firedancer or the Green Genie showing up in town beating on muggers or breaking up a bank robbery because they're tryin' to build a rep before auditioning for the Brigade. Some of them probably really was all civic-minded, but most of them were after the money and publicity, and everyone knew the Brigade was well-funded. Most folks thought it was still government.

Anyway. That's more or less where things were in '62 when Ghostwalker came on the scene. Nobody knew what the hell *his* story was. It started with guys getting dropped off at the police station—small-timers, muggers and whatnot—all tied up with a note saying what crime they did, signed with a little ghost cartoon saying BOO! Like this, gimme that pen, I can sketch it for you.

Nutty, right? But the *seriously* weird part is that these guys, they're already tied up and had the stuffing knocked out of 'em, bruised and bleeding, you'd think they'd be all pissed off and screaming about their rights. That's how it usually went when the mask-and-cape crowd pulled that shit. Sure, it's dramatic, made the papers, but the part that got left out is those gift-wrapped crooks all *walked* unless they were wanted for something else. Trussing 'em up and dropping 'em at the station an' then taking off like that, it just wasted everyone's time. Cops were never able to hold 'em. None of them union-suit characters ever would unmask and take it all the way to court. So vigilante busts like that, half the time cops never bothered booking 'em.

But the ones the ghost guy dropped off were different. They couldn't confess fast enough. They were terrified. *Please lock me up, it's the only way I'll be safe.* That's how it always went. They'd confess to stuff going back years, never mind what they did that night. And all they'd say about the guy what bagged 'em was that he wasn't human.

He was mostly working the docks and the bad neighborhoods down by Goldwater Beach—not far from the Liberty Mission, actually. People started to catch glimpses of him, there were a couple of fuzzy newspaper pics, things like that. Pretty soon folks started callin' him Ghostwalker and it stuck. Dressed all in gray, full face mask with a hood, and something that was either a cape or a robe or something, kinda swirling around him. That was all anybody knew. No weapons anyone ever saw but he could take out five or eight guys at a time just with his fists, in a fight it was like he was everywhere at once. Street crooks thought he was magic or something supernatural. News guys were floating all kinds of theories… One guy over at the PBS affiliate was absolutely convinced it was Devilhound who'd faked his own death and this was his comeback. I coulda told him it wasn't, because I was there when Devilhound bought it and *nobody* comes back from that… but that's another story.

Ghostwalker had everybody talking, that's my point. No possibility too weird for St. Jacques back then. You know, you already got a city full of superpowered people, nothing's off the table any more.

But Ghostwalker wasn't any of the things people were saying. I found out the hard way.

It started with Trav—you remember him, he was my broker, the guy what lined up jobs for me. We had a pretty intricate system worked out where people who needed their lair done or their laser guns recalibrated or whatever could get word to us, there was a drop box—not a P.O. box, an office down by Kincannon Square. Vacant, I never went there, it didn't even have furniture. It was just a place with a mail slot in the door and some bullshit name on the pebbled glass over it. But I rigged a secret entrance where Trav came up in an elevator from the sewer system underneath the building, and I had hidden cameras in the hall rigged to a motion sensor. The infrared see-in-the-dark kind, I mean. But mine were—well, never mind, I can see I lost you already. I get carried away talking about the technical part of things.

It was just a place with a mail slot in the door...

What I mean is, Trav and I had it worked out where no one knew how to get to me unless I let 'em. There was two things I paid him for. First was to keep his ear to the ground for guys needed my kind of skills. What you might call extra-legal engineering. Second was to get word to 'em that they could send a note to the drop box explaining what they were after and I'd get in touch. Maybe. No guarantees. If it looked like something I could do—and it wasn't always, some of those guys wanted really crazy shit like a headquarters on an orbiting asteroid or something. But if it was something I could do, y'know, down here on Earth, I'd get back to 'em, or Trav would, we'd work out a price, and then I'd get into it. Once it was done I'd collect my fee and say so long and leave 'em to their big mad-science scheme. Mostly they'd crash and burn and end up doing hard time, some super'd swoop in and smash it all to hell. But by then I was long gone, off to the next one.

I see you giving me the eye. What?

Look, I *know* it was crooked. Of course it was. People got hurt from what I built, no question. But it was so much money… and we needed that money for Debbie, it wasn't like I was being greedy. She was already getting sick with the leukemia that finally got her. You want to talk about greedy; you shoulda' seen the hospital bills we were getting hit with. So don't be getting on your high horse about drawing the line till you're up against it like we were. Then you find out where your real line is. Mine was Debbie. Period the end.

I'm losing track of my story here. Oh yeah, the drop. Well, Trav and I used to meet at the tavern down the block from my apartment, little place called the Clover. Irish pub, like, that was their deal. Not really upscale but nice, lots of teak and brass and no band or jukebox or anything, you could just sit and have your beer in peace. They did a great roast beef sandwich too. We usually met there on Tuesdays.

Anyway, one Tuesday Trav comes in with a nervous expression and says, "I got a weird one. Lot of money but I don't know if you want it."

"I always want a lot of money. You know they got this bone marrow thing they want to try for Debbie. Let's have it."

Trav hands me the note. It says, *We are aware of your skills from various contacts of ours in the superhuman community. We need a man of your talent and discretion for a job that pays $10,000 on completion. But we must meet in person. Midnight, Thursday the 9th, Longmeadows Park, by the fountain.*

Two days. I shrugged and handed it back to him. "So?"

"Sounds hinky to me." Trav shook his head. "Like a setup."

"Like cops, you mean?" I snorted. "Cops even don't know we exist. Guys like you and me, we're just henching it. They want the headliners, not the support crew."

"Not cops. I was thinking Brigade maybe. You know Liberty Jane was on Jack Paar talking about urban cancer and whatever…"

I waved it off. "Naw. What this is, this is a guy who doesn't want to pay. 'On completion' is a dead giveaway. He thinks I'll build him his whatever and then he'll stiff me and what am I gonna do, sue him? Well, I dealt with his kind before and I still got paid. I know how to handle these guys, don't worry. You just gotta be ready for when they try and knife you." I grinned. "Not a problem. Ten grand's too big not to at least take a look. I'll go. But…" I winked at him. "I'll be ready. Rest your mind. Hard part's going to be explaining being out so late to Debbie, that's all. But I managed that before too."

Trav nodded, still looking uneasy.

If I'd known what was coming, I'd'a been uneasy too. But at that point it was only a job, one more super-widget for one more super-weirdo. Just another day at the office for me.

◉◉◉

I tried never to out-n-out lie to Debbie. I just left stuff out so she wouldn't worry. She was a good Methodist girl and she wouldn't a'liked me working for crooks, even though I wasn't committing no crimes. Well, not technically, anyway. I mean, it's not illegal to build stuff. Though I gotta admit we kinda' skirted the edges when it came to zoning and OSHA laws and such, and I think it's probably some kind of crime if you're knowingly doing business with somebody on the Ten Most Wanted list.

But mostly, everything *I* did as Doc Fixit, I made sure I was in the clear. I had incorporated as a small business, I made sure I got paid by cashier's check so's I'd have a paper trail for the IRS—yeah, I paid taxes. I mean, come on. I'd risk my neck working for Steel Spectre, sure, but only a damn fool plays footsie with the tax man. And doing it that way, it worked same as cash, clients wouldn't have anything leading to them, so they didn't get nervous on their end. I tried to think of everything. I was always—*always*—damn careful. Just because my customers were mental cases in weird suits don't mean they weren't *dangerous*.

But there was no point in burdening my Debbie with all of that. "Got to meet a guy and look at some work he wants done," I told her. "I'm afraid I'm gonna be late. Might end up being a month or two of night work if I take it."

"Oh, Ernie." She gave me a hug. "You work too hard."

"We need the money, you know we do." I pulled her close and kissed her, and let my chin rest on the top of her head for a moment. Then I pulled back and looked at her. "Don't you worry about me. How you feeling? Them pills helping?"

"Some. I don't like them, though, they make me all draggy."

"I don't like you hurting." I scowled. "You take one if you need to. There ain't no points for being all heroic. This ain't a movie and you ain't John Wayne."

"I know." She sighed and for a moment she looked so bleak and sad I got a lump in my throat like I might start crying.

Instead I swallowed it back and said, "Anyway, I gotta get out to meet this guy. Don't wait up."

"Eat something. Something healthy," she added, and this smile wasn't bleak. "Not those greasy burgers from the drive-in."

"All right. For you I'll get a salad at the deli." I kissed her and went.

Okay, that was a little lie I told, yeah, but it made Debbie happy so screw it. Truth is, I didn't go to the deli. Eating made me sleepy and for a first meet I needed to be sharp.

Instead I drove to the outskirts of Longmeadows and suited up. I didn't have a costume, but I had what I called my work clothes. Basic mechanic's coverall. Black electrician's gloves, thin cloth with rubber-coated fingers. Tool belt with a couple of useful electronic gizmos tucked away in the pouches along with my screwdriver and hammer and wrenches. And my goggles I'd rigged special, that also served to hide my face some. Nothing that said *costumed crook* to any cop that happened by and I had a story for any that did. But in my work duds I was as dangerous as any supervillain, if I needed to be.

I parked a ways away from the fountain, left my wallet and ID locked in the car, and walked the rest of the way. Slow approach, checking it out. I tapped the side of my goggles, activating the night vision.

The guy waiting by the fountain was standing ramrod straight, briefcase in hand, dressed in a business suit and wearing a gray fedora hat. He would have looked like a banker or something except for two things; the briefcase was chained to his wrist and he was wearing a black domino mask.

He heard me coming up on him and turned to face me with a thin smile showing no teeth. "Ah. Doctor Fixit? I see you are dressed for work." Faint British accent. Definitely a limey but one who'd been living here in the States for a while.

"I'm a working guy."

"Indeed." The smile got a little wider, a little thinner, but still no teeth. "I have ten thousand dollars in bearer bonds in this briefcase. If we come to terms I unlock the cuff chaining it to my wrist and it's all yours. Shall we discuss the job?"

"First let's discuss your pal over there." I nodded towards the other side of the fountain. "That's a good screen but I'm not some mugger. I done light-bending work myself, I know an invisibility shimmer when I see it." I admit I was bluffing a little. It was the night-vision infrared in my goggles what put me on to him; no matter how good your holograms are, they can't hide your heat signature. But it was better to keep 'em guessing. "I don't have time for games. He's hanging back so I'm guessing he's the boss. Let's talk face to face if we're going to talk business. Like I said, I'm a working guy and it's past my bedtime." I looked past the limey and addressed the shimmer. "I'm here like you asked. Let's get to it."

A new voice came, layered on top of itself with lots of reverb. "Clearly, your reputation is deserved."

It sounded spooky, yeah, but I knew what a throat mic was. This guy was strictly science-based, no superpowers that I could see. This was all stage-magic stuff.

Proving my point, there was a swirl of smoke and then there he was. I was getting probably the first good look at him anyone ever had, thanks to my goggles. Hooded, with a full face mask, and white orbs where his eyes should be. Some kinda opaque lenses. What people said was a cape or a robe was really a long gray silk coat, same cut as a leather duster, with sleeves that got wide at the end. He was wearing gloves, a little darker gray than the coat and the mask.

I blinked. "You're the boo boy from the papers. Ghostwalker, right?"

He nodded and pointed at me. "And you are the famous Doc Fixit."

I started to get a little nervous. "Yeah. I gotta say, I don't usually get calls from your side of the street."

"Is that going to be a problem?" Whatever enhancements he'd used with the mic, it really was a damn spooky voice. That and the smoke made it a convincing act.

Just tech, I reminded myself. *Don't let him rattle you.* "No problem here," I tried to keep the quaver out of my voice. "So what's the job? Are you here to do business or not?"

"We'll do business. But not here." Ghostwalker waved his hand again and everything around me started to shimmer. Not optics this time. Son of a bitch was using gas. *Some kind of mist pump on his back, hose runs down the sleeve and spray nozzles built into the gloves,* I thought, blearily. Even passing out, I was still thinking like an engineer.

Black crept in around the edges of my vision and I had the distant sensation I was falling forward, but I was out before I hit the ground.

◉◉◉

I came to in a white room with no windows. I could hear the faint whooshing sound of a ventilation system but with no vents I could see. Normally when somebody gasses you, you wake up with the mother of all hangovers. But I felt okay. Just a little weak and shaky. Whatever he was using, it was the good stuff. High-end, KGB level. I knew our military didn't have chemicals that sophisticated but the Russians did. I hoped to Christ this wasn't some international thing. I didn't mind helping out the bank robbers and so on but political stuff was guaranteed trouble.

"Doctor?" The limey's voice.

I sat up and rubbed my eyes. I was still in my work outfit, but they'd taken the goggles and the tool belt. I was on a cot set against one wall of the white room. Featureless except for a door set flush in the wall at the far end.

I saw the limey leaning on a workbench against the wall on the opposite side from me. He'd shucked the jacket and fedora, but still was in the shirt and tie. And of course the domino mask.

"Where's my stuff?" I asked him.

"Right here." He moved aside and I could see my belt and goggles on the workbench behind him. "Everything is intact. We were concerned about some kind of homing tracker, because we need this location to remain secret."

"You think I can't keep secrets? For Chrissake, d'you think I'd have lasted as long as I have without keeping my trap shut? I know stuff about folks you wouldn't..."

He held up a hand. "I believe you. Truly." He paused for a moment and looked almost embarrassed. Then he went on, more firmly, "But we intend to last as well, however, and you must understand that means taking precautions. We had to be sure you weren't carrying anything that broadcast a signal. If we can put this initial awkwardness behind us, I assure you, we still want to hire you."

I jabbed a finger at him. "I got conditions. You better hear me out before we go any further."

He nodded and gestured for me to go ahead.

"Okay." I drew in a long breath and let it out slow. "First, you never gas me again. Blindfold, bag over the head, whatever, I ain't interested in where you hide your secret headquarters. But no gas."

"Of course…"

"I mean fear gas too."

He blinked and I could see the startled expression even behind his mask.

I snorted and went on, "For God's sake. Your guy must be spoiled dealing with muggers and small-timers. Get it through your head, I been *around*, all right? I know the tricks. I could feel whatever he uses working on me before he let loose the sleepy stuff. Nozzles in the gloves, right? Some kind of…. I dunno, I'm not a chemical engineer. But it works on the fight-or-flight response, got to be something like that. Some kinda nerve agent."

The limey was looking at me with new respect. "Indeed. You are very astute."

"I was already thinking it must be something like that from the news stories." I waved it away. "It's not new. Steel Spectre used to use a gimmick like that, but his was mechanical. Subsonics. We could never lick the power curve on it, though, so he only was able… never mind. That's not the point. The point is, if we are going to do business, you treat me with some goddamn *respect*. I'm not some ignorant stickup man. I'm a professional. Save the spook act for the rubes."

The door at the far end of the room opened and Ghostwalker strode in. Still all suited up, but he didn't bother with the smoke effects this time. "Very well, Doctor," he said. No reverb in it. *He must have been listening in*, I thought, and it was confirmed when he added, "Those conditions are acceptable."

"I ain't done." I glared at him.

"Oh?" Ghostwalker crossed his arms and nodded at me to continue. He sounded amused. Beside him, the masked limey was looking a little nervous.

I ignored it. This was a job and I was a pro. "You want to keep your secrets. I understand that. I'm going to need some things, though. Whatever you want done, if you called me, it means there's going to be some serious engineering involved, right? Metalworking, electronics, machining parts probably, who knows what-all. You got ways to get that stuff here? We working on-site? Because if I have to figure out all that too, it's going to mean more money. Not just for me, I mean basic capital expenditure." I shrugged. "On the other hand, you just want a consult, I'm happy to take a look, but I'm thinking ten grand means hands-on. So ten grand's probably just the beginning. It ain't just me that's gonna cost you."

Ghostwalker nodded. "A reasonable assessment." He turned to the limey. "I think he'll do. See to the details." He spun around without waiting for an answer and swept out of the room.

The door closed with a soft click and I chuckled. "Well. He's a little full of himself, ain't he? But I guess all these costume guys are." I faced the limey. "Where do you fit in to all this, anyway? You been working for him all along?"

"I suppose you could say I once had your job." He smiled a little ruefully at me. "I'm something of an engineer myself, but...." He held out a hand and I could see it trembling. "My health doesn't permit me to do the fine detail work the way I used to."

I winced. "Palsy?"

"Technically it's called Parkinson's Disease. There is no cure." He sighed. "It's not too bad. Eventually I will be in a wheelchair, I imagine, but for now, I can manage... for the most part. My intellect is not hampered. I can't use my hands the way I used to, that's all. So much of the work I do here involves concealment and miniaturization. I can't do the subtle things any more." Again with the rueful smile. "So I persuaded the master to let me hire some help. I realize our approach was a bit unconventional, and perhaps discourteous, but...."

"It's the business we're in. I get it." I kinda liked him, I decided. His boss mighta been a jerk but this Brit seemed like a decent guy. "Fair enough. Let's talk about the job. But if we're going to be working together, I'd just as soon use real names. You can call me Ernie."

That was the first time I got a genuine smile out of him, one with teeth. He reached up and took off his mask. "All right. I'm Alastair."

"Nice to meetcha." We shook hands. "So what's the job?"

"Ah, that will involve some explaining. If you can follow me..."

I stood up. "First you gotta let me call my wife. She's gonna wonder why I ain't home yet. I don't care if you listen in but no trace, okay?"

"No trace. My word." Alastair flashed me another smile. "We won't trouble the master with it. After all, we are both professionals."

With that, I knew he was my kinda guy, in spite of the plummy accent.

When you're henching, you get a feel for what stuff you tell the boss and what stuff you don't bother him about. I guess it worked that way on the hero side of things too.

He gestured at the workbench for me to reclaim my tool belt and goggles. I put 'em back on and checked the pouches on the belt. Everything there. I pushed the goggles back up on my head and nodded at Alastair. "Okay. Phone?"

He led me out through the door to a white hallway, lit with fluorescents. Like in an office building, but a little too bright. He pointed at a small alcove and I saw a phone sitting there. White too, of course. "Dial 9 to get an outside line."

I nodded and picked up the handset. "How long has it been, anyway? What time is it now?"

Alaistair consulted a pocket watch. The guy was an old-fashioned Brit to his toes. "A little after five AM."

"Okay." I hated waking her up but I knew if Debbie woke up on her own with me not there, she'd be in a panic. I moved to where my back was to Alastair and dialed. Standing that way he couldn't see me palm a silver disc from my front belt pouch and slide it under the phone. When I felt the magnet click into place I felt better. I liked the guy but that didn't mean I trusted him, not yet. And I sure didn't trust his boss. Insurance never hurts.

I heard the burr of the phone ringing on Debbie's end. She picked up right away. Damn it, she must have been waiting up. "Ernie, is that you? Are you all right?"

"I'm fine, honey, just checking in. This is taking longer than I thought it would, that's all."

"I'm glad to hear from you. I was worried,"

"I know. I'm sorry. Time got away from me." I glanced at Alastair. He had the grace to look embarrassed. "Anyway, it all looks fine. I think the job's going to work out. Shouldn't be too much longer. You should go back to bed."

"I can't sleep till you get here."

"At least try. For me."

"All right." She added, "You worry about me all the time, I'm allowed to worry about you too."

"Nothing to worry about. It's just another job. You go to bed now. I love you."

"I love you too. Be safe."

I hung up and turned to face Alastair. "Okay?"

He nodded, his expression looking a little wistful. "It's for her, isn't it? The work you do, the risks you take. She must be something special."

"She is." I was curt. I didn't want to talk about Debbie. So I diverted. "What about your guy? How'd you get mixed up with him?"

Alastair could divert too. He sighed. "Oh we all make our devil's bargain, I suppose. Anyway, come along, let's take a look at the work you're here for." He led us to the end of the hall through another door, this one heavier-duty than the others. Then he turned and gestured for me to precede him. I shrugged and went on through.

It was bigger than a garage but smaller than a hangar, and it looked like it could function as either. Concrete floor and corrugated metal siding on all sides, with two big doors at one end. Still no windows, just lots of racks and machinery and tools. In the center was something that looked like a car, or at least the skeleton of a car, with an engine hanging from a crane over the front and various pieces of the chassis sort of scattered around it, all the same cloud-gray as Ghostwalker's outfit. Off to one side I could see another workbench piled high with electronics and wiring.

Suddenly I got it. "Oh man," I breathed, and my face lit up with this big grin like a kid in a candy store.

"What?" Alastair had looked startled at first, then wryly amused. "Is something funny?"

"Your boss," I chuckled. "He's just a big kid underneath all the spook-show act. He wants a tricked-out rod. Right? All this cloak-and-dagger for a cool car?"

Alastair harrumphed. "I have designed it to be the ultimate stealth urban operational vehicle, infinitely maneuverable with multiple defense and offense capabilities." One corner of his mouth pulled up in another thin-lipped smile. "But yes, with your help, Doctor—Ernie—I expect the Ghost-mobile shall be a *very* cool car."

◉◉◉

It didn't take long to work out a routine. We met weeknights around ten, Longmeadows Park, same as the first time. Alastair'd pick me up in a limo, and I'd get in the back. He'd roll up the privacy screen and pull out. Windows were blacked out so no need for sleep gas, though I had my nose filters in all the time anyway. Fool me once and all that. But there was never any trouble or tricks.

I have to admit this was my favorite kinda job to work on. I always was a car guy, and this kind of hands-on labor was hugely relaxing for me: something like this took my mind off Debbie being so sick, I could just get lost in the job. Believe it or not, in all my years as Doc Fixit, this was the first time I'd ever actually got to work on a real car. Subs, hovercraft, even tanks, sure. But never just a cool car. I guess underneath it all I was a big kid too.

It was great to get in there with my tools and build this thing. Alastair's blueprints were very thorough; he'd already solved most of the practical problems at the design stage. The guy was just brilliant, that's all there was to it. Damn shame about the palsy, but even with that he coulda wrote his own ticket at any of the big outfits. Boeing, Lockheed, hell, he coulda retired at forty just on the patents for things he'd figured out for this supercar.

But then, in our line of work, patents weren't really a factor. I suppose you could say the same thing about me. I guess I coulda got out of the business if I really tried. I didn't have a college degree and my proudest accomplishments as an engineer were for stuff I couldn't a'never put on a legit employment application. But I might have gone legit if I'd put my mind to it. The thing is, me and Debbie were always just kinda living from one medical panic to the next, and I already had a solution that was working. Why rock the boat?

Alastair's designs were seriously next-level stuff, though. I couldn't see why he'd play second fiddle to a nut in a ghost outfit. The few times I'd asked him about it, he brushed me off the same way I'd done him with talking about Debbie. Well, fair enough. People in the business always had reasons. I had mine, he had his. Whatever. I let it go.

I wasn't really worrying, not at first. This gets lost in all the news reports about the supers and the villains, but the work I was doing, well… it was *fun*. This Ghostwalker job especially. I mean, the job was to basically build the world's coolest car, right? How can you not love that? Also, I hardly ever got to work with someone that was on my level, but Alastair was…. I gotta be honest here. He was better than me. I was learning a lot. The things he had doped out about miniaturization…

Look. You gotta understand, in the late fifties, early sixties, it was always a war between power and portability. It doesn't matter if you got a raygun that can carve up a bank vault if the generator running it is so huge you can't even get it loaded into a pickup. The power demands go sky-high for that kind of thing and all these villain guys were after something handheld. I'd tried all kinds of things over the years, solar chargers, mirror-stacked laser remotes, any kind of crackpot notion that could give you a lot of juice that didn't draw off the city grid, something you could pick up and take with you.

The Ghostmobile was kinda that problem, but doubled down, because we had to run a car engine along with all the weapons systems. And we had to do it without weighing it down so heavy that it'd never go faster'n twenty miles an hour. I don't know if I'd have ever figured it out on my own, but Alastair's solution was elegant. Once we got to work on it I realized it wasn't a car engine at all. "This is like a jet," I said. "A plane, but with wheels instead of wings?"

"After a fashion." Alastair looked pleased. "Except we don't burn fuel. Batteries are charged from the miniature atomic pile and the intakes up front bring in the air to spin the turbines. We have a brief pause for the initial power-up but then it should run for days without any need to recharge." His brow furrowed. "Honestly the difficulty is reining it in. It's vastly overpowered for regular street driving, and masking the hoverjet noise has been deeply frustrating."

"We can't get the turbines any quieter." I considered it. "You already got the chassis configured almost like a wing, the faster it goes the more lift the car gets, so there's that much less power demand on the engine. Get it up on plane like a speedboat, almost. That helps a little. Highway's no problem, it's city driving you have to worry about. Maybe add a set of baffles to the exhaust, or even some kind of sonic array... I don't know the word for it. White sound, I think they called it when I was figuring out Steel Spectre's death maze. He had kind of a ghost schtick too, so he was all about keeping his gizmos quiet. There's a trick with sonics where you find frequencies what cancel each other out, like." I scowled. "I wish I'd wrote that stuff down back then, but you know how these guys get about paper trails. Still..."

A new voice broke in. "Hey, Al, who's the new guy?"

The voice was coming from what I thought at first was some kind of Ghostwalker stunt double, a masked-and-costumed kid that sounded no older than nineteen or twenty. But on second look there were differences between his look and Ghostwalker's. His outfit was a little tighter, almost like something a gymnast would wear, and the hood didn't cover his whole head, the top was cut off so you could see tousled brown hair. The eyes were the same kind of white opaque lenses, but the swirly cape thing really was a cape, not a jacket, with the ends attached at the wrists. He looked more like a circus aerialist than anything. But his outfit was definitely patterned after Ghostwalker.

"I'm Ernie," I said. "And you are?"

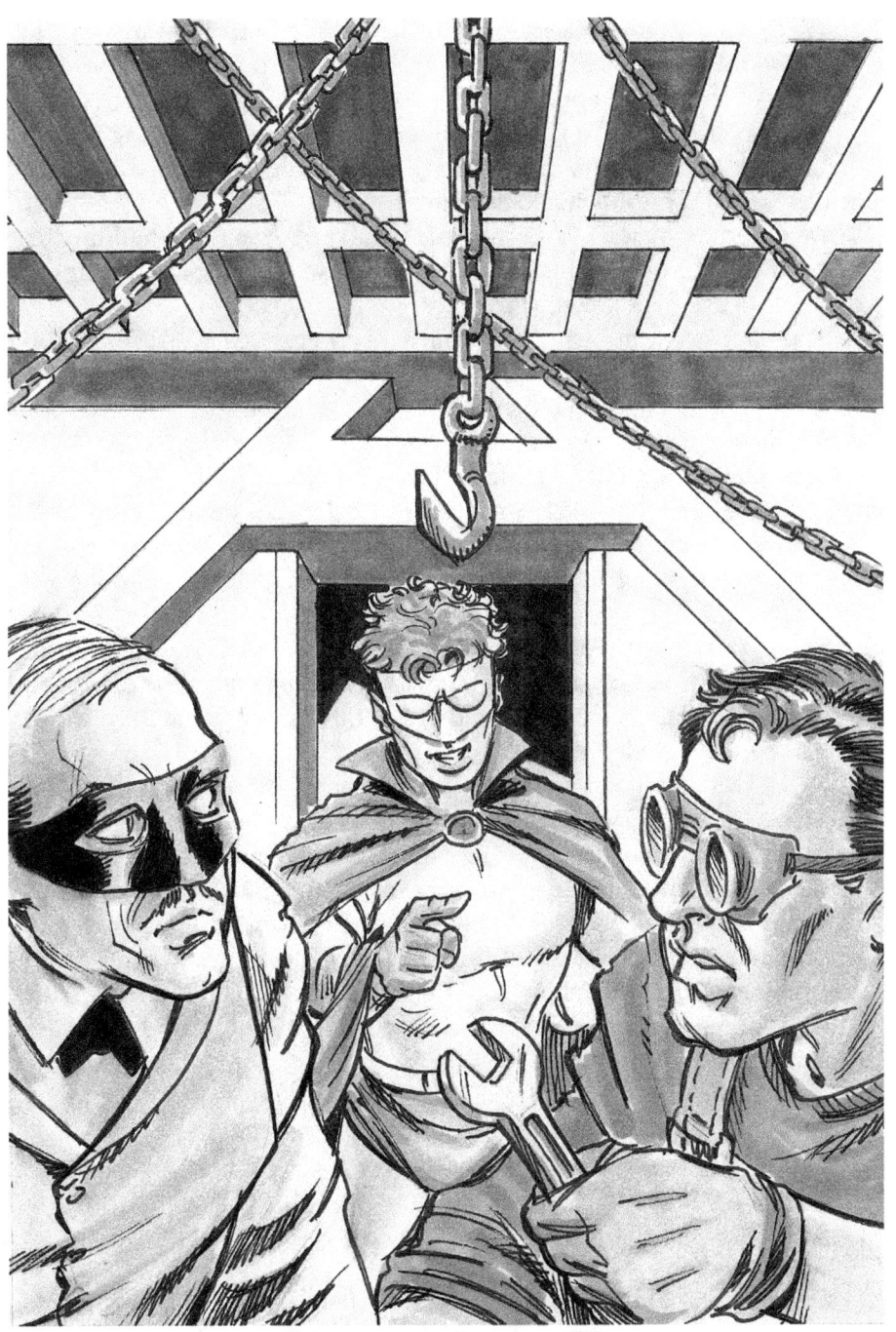

"Hey, Al, who's the new guy?"

"Code names only," Alastair put in before the kid could answer. He turned to me and smiled apologetically. "You understand, of course. This young man is my ward and I'm charged with his safety."

I could hear the kid snort and I imagine his eyes were rolling behind the mask. "You worry too much, Al. All right. Code names it is. That was actually why I came down, tell the truth."

Down. I filed that away in the little mental dossier I was building on this outfit. I'd suspected this garage-workshop-whatever space was underground. Nice to have it confirmed.

Alastair crossed his arms and smiled wryly at the kid. "We're back to this?"

"I'm not calling myself Ghost Boy."

"We have to call you something,"

"How about Kid Ghost?" I asked. "Like a boxer."

"Hmmm." Alastair looked at me, interested. "That is better, I must say."

But the caped kid just made a noise of frustration. "That's not the point. I don't want anything about Boy or Kid in the name *at all.* I'm not a kid any more, Al."

"Until you're twenty-one you are, and under my care." Alaistair's voice had the tiniest little edge in it. "You insist on accompanying the master on his patrols, despite my objections. There's little I can do about it, seeing as how he has approved. But…"

I could tell Alastair was getting a little lost in the weeds, and the moment was getting awkward. I decided to rescue them both from the family quarrel it was shaping up to become. "Look here," I said to the kid. "You're making too much of it. The name don't matter that much as long as folks remember you. Call yourself Spookster or Revenant or Gravedigger or whatever. You don't want to get mixed up with anybody else is all. So I'd leave out anything with 'ghost' in it, save that one for your partner. Same with 'spectre,' because a' Steel Spectre. But there's lotsa' other ghostly names out there. Just pick one."

"Gravedigger sounds kinda cool," the kid admitted.

"And it's got assonance," Alaistair added.

"What?" The kid sounded confused.

"Rhythm," I told him. "Ghostwalker and Gravedigger. Both start with G, both end with R, three syllables each. You get words what pair up like that but don't rhyme, it's called assonance."

"Hey, you're right. That's pretty smart." There was new respect in the kid's voice. Then it became rueful. "Not paired up tonight, though. Big guy benched me."

"Oh?" I said, innocently. Small talk, but I was always looking to add to the dossier. Like I said, in my business, liking folks has nothing to do with trusting 'em.

Alastair shot him a warning look but it sailed right by the kid. "Yeah, he said he was going after Serpentina. Too dangerous for me."

"That's enough, young man." Alastair's voice had an edge in it. "Run along upstairs and get out of that uniform, since you're not going out." His voice softened a little. "I'll be along in a bit. We can talk about design improvements to reflect your new name."

"Okay, Al. Sounds good." The kid bounded out. He moved like a human spring, energy just came off him in waves.

"Thank you for that," Alastair said to me after the kid was gone. "The young master is somewhat irrepressible."

"Ain't nothing," I said, but I was only half-listening. My mind was in a whirl.

Tina? What the hell did this spookshow outfit want with Tina?

◎◎◎

I knew Serpentina, see. Got acquainted with her back in the Devilhound days. She'd been part of the Reptile Squad, Lizard King's outfit. But she saw what a creep he turned out to be and jumped ship over to Devilhound's gang while I was doing his lair, and we got to be friends. Mostly because I was the only guy there that wasn't putting the make on her. She was a knockout—the best kind of pretty, the kind where she doesn't hardly even know it. No vanity to her.

Her schtick was climbing—not a super, just a world-class gymnast, 'cept the whole city was her parallel bars, like. You shoulda' seen her slither up a fire escape and whip across an alley five stories up, going from a flagpole to a window ledge to a chimney like it was nothing. She was Olympic material, easy. I helped her out a bit back in the day; fixed her up with a little collapsible grapnel line she could wear on her belt, and gloves with vacuum suction for going up glass-front skyscrapers, which were starting to be a thing here starting around '58. Nice kid. But she'd quit Devilhound about the same time I did, and I heard she went straight. Even in her heyday she wasn't any kind of real danger to folks, her thing was burglary. Jewels were her specialty but she was good with industrial espionage too.

I couldn't figure out why Ghostwalker was chasing her but I thought it wouldn't hurt to give her a heads-up. Tina wasn't really equipped to take on a heavy hitter like him, especially with his fear gas gimmick.

I thought finding her might be a problem but all it took was a phone call to Trav. He kept tabs on folks; that was one of the things I paid him for. Networking, I guess you kids call it now. Course it helped I knew her real name. All most hoods knew was "Serpentina" but I knew she was really just Tina Jankewicz from the South side.

Debbie usually napped in the afternoon after she took her pills, so I told her I was going to run a couple of errands. I did need to pick up some thin high-tension cable, just a little spool of the stuff. Alastair and I were playing with an idea for a sort of electric-net gun we could mount on the front of the Ghostmobile. Alastair was adamant we stick with non-lethal hardware, and I remembered the tanglewire trap I'd figured out for the Midnight Midas. Just had to figure out how to mount the—well, never mind all that. But it gave me an excuse to be out and around and it wasn't any trouble to stop by Tina's place after.

It turned out to be a fourth-floor walkup not too far from the riverfront, only about ten blocks or so from Longmeadows as it turned out. Kinda run-down, but clean. Climbing the stairs I could hear kids laughing and old guys arguing and all sorts of stuff; walls musta' been paper-thin. The smell of boiled cabbage permeated the hallway. Reminded me of Debbie's and my first place back in '49, before I fell into the Doc Fixit thing and we was able to buy a house.

When Tina opened the door her eyes went wide and her face split in a delighted grin. She wrapped me in a big hug. "Ernie! Oh my God it's been years. Come in, come in. How are you? How's your wife?"

We made small talk for a couple of minutes. There's always the uncomfortable part where I had to explain about Debbie being sick. Not going into all kinds of detail or anything, but you gotta tell people something. So I gave her the short version that made it sound better than it was, then added, "Truth is, kid, I ain't here just to catch up. I want you to tell me the truth, now. You back in the business?"

Tina looked away for a second. Now it was her that was uncomfortable. Finally she said, "Sort of. I mean, it's going to just be a one-off, but… God, Ernie, I'm so embarrassed. I've made such a mess of things. I don't even know where to start."

"You know this Ghostwalker guy is gunning for you."

That shocked her, but not the way I thought. "How did you know about him? That was just a few nights… oh, hell." Then she busted out crying.

I felt like an idiot. I don't know what I was thinking would happen but this wasn't it. I just held her and said stupid things like *Hey*, and *It's gonna be all right*, until the storm passed.

Finally she pushed me away and went to sit on an old overstuffed couch. "Boy, if the Reptiles could see me now." She let out a bitter laugh.

"What is it, honey?" I asked her. "What's up with Ghostwalker? He trying to send you up? Some kind of publicity bust? You been out of the game for a while, what's the point?"

Tina shook her head. "He's blackmailing me."

"What? How? What's he got on you?"

Then the bedroom door opened and a voice said, "Mommy? I heard voices." A little curly-headed blonde girl in a pink jumper emerged from the bedroom.

"Hi sweetie, I hope you had a nice nap." Tina smiled wanly and added, "This is Sarah, Ernie. My daughter."

So then I knew exactly what Ghostwalker had on her. One phone call to the feds and Sarah loses her mommy. With that to hold over Tina's head, he owned her.

◉◉◉

I ended up bringing Tina and her daughter back home with me for dinner. "The spook won't find you at our place, and Debbie'd love to see you. It'll be a break for you and it buys me some time to figure out how to help you. Just remember," I added, "No work talk, at dinner, y'know what I mean? Far as Debbie's concerned I'm in construction, engineering. Contract work."

That got another bitter laugh out of Tina. "Well, it's true, isn't it?"

"Exactly."

Dinner turned out to be a good call for everybody. Debbie was more herself than she'd been for months, with Tina and especially little Sarah to fuss over. My wife loved kids, it was a damn crime she wasn't able to have any.

We had a spare room with a sofa, and other odds and ends. Kind of a craft room; it was mostly where Debbie did her sewing. My wife had it all figured out. She told Tina, "We can put you on the couch and the little one can make do on the floor. Like camping, but inside, right sweetie?" This last was to Sarah.

"Yay, camping!" Sarah was all over that. Debbie laughed, her first real laugh in a year, I think. And even Tina giggled.

After dinner I gave Debbie the high sign that she should take Sarah out of the room so Tina and I could talk. So she and Sarah went back to the spare room to liven up the camping festivities with more refinements. "Blanket fort, I think," Debbie said.

"What's a blanket fort?" Sarah wanted to know.

"The best thing ever," Debbie assured her, and they disappeared back into the craft room.

I raised an eyebrow at Tina. "You look like you could stand to hide out in a blanket fort yourself, kid."

"I miss life being simple. Even in the old days, climbing buildings and running from cops and all, it was still just me. A kid comes into your life and everything changes." She sighed. "I wouldn't trade Sarah for the world, but it's not just me, alone, any more, you know? I have to think through everything."

"Her dad's not in the picture at all, then."

"Not since '59." Tina's smile was wan. "Ricky was smart and handsome and fun, but not really daddy material. Met him when we were both Reptile Guard. He stayed when I left and it all just kind of fell apart. There was no way we were going to get married. He did send us money, he might have come around to going domestic with us, but he got killed in that big showdown at the Mint." She shrugged. "I don't hold a grudge. It's who he was. It's been me and Sarah against the world all along. I'm used to it."

"Does Sarah know?"

"Just that he's gone. I told her he died on the job. Accident. It's true enough. The rest can wait till she's older." She sighed and smiled at me. "I guess that's the kind of smoothed-over truth you tell Debbie, huh?"

"Kind of." This was a road I didn't want to go down. "So how'd you get back into the life?"

"I didn't." Tina's eyes flashed with anger. "It's that Ghost bastard, he's pushing me back in."

"What does he want?"

"He wants me to knock off Reichenbach Motors. Simple really, office safe with plans, but it's in a penthouse. Locked off from the main building, private elevator. It's an industrial job. You know, they're the ones that…"

"That make the fancy sports cars," I finished.

She nodded.

I had that feeling you get when you're looking at a big engineering problem, something with a lot of moving parts but you can't get it solved because there's a couple things you can't see. I turned the pieces around in my head, trying to figure how they fit. Burglary. Supers. A hero that maybe wasn't. Using a villain proxy. And this supercar me and Alistair were building. It all fit together, somehow, I knew it did, but I couldn't see it. Not quite.

"You kids should stay here for a couple days," I told her. "Buy you some time away from Big Bad Boo. Let me see if I can get a handle on this for you."

I thought she was gonna fight me on it, but she agreed with relief. Ghost-walker really had her wound up tight. I was pretty sure there was stuff she hadn't told me but I wasn't gonna lean on her when she was so obviously terrified. Instead, I got up to go get my work duds on. It was getting time to get myself over to Longmeadows to meet Alastair and the limo.

Debbie came out to join us and as she came to me, Tina went back to the craft room to see how Sarah was doing. Debbie smiled at her over her shoulder and then put her arms around my waist and turned to me. "That's a sweet little girl. Both of them are."

"Tina was always a good kid. Just had some bad luck."

Debbie looked up at me with steel in her eyes. I knew that look. She'd made up her mind. "We need to help them, Ernie."

That was my girl. Once she'd decided you were family, it was ride or die all the way. "I'm going to do what I can," I told her.

"It's a man, isn't it? Poor little girl, raising a daughter all alone, she's easy prey. No, I don't need to know the details. She needs a break from worrying about it. And you need to run along to work, mister." She gave my butt an affectionate pat. "You can tell me everything later."

"Will do." I grinned at her and went back to the bedroom to get my coveralls. *Maybe I really should tell her everything,* I thought for the millionth time. *One of these days I will.*

◉◉◉

In spite of everything I was excited to get back to Alastair and the garage that night because we were about ready for the first test run. The car was built and we'd figured on taking it out to the hills east of town and seeing what it could really do.

I should have known better.

I could tell something was off from when Alastair picked me up. I said something about finally the big night being here and all he did was grunt. British gentlemen don't grunt; Alastair *never* grunted. So I knew something was up. But, you know, in the trade, we don't ask questions. I figured it was another family squabble over the kid and forgot about it.

I almost had it right. The awkward squabble between the spook and Alastair wasn't about Junior. Apparently it had been about me.

When we arrived and I got out of the blacked out limo, the garage was mostly dark except for a small circle of light next to the completed Ghost-mobile. In the center of the circle stood Ghostwalker, in his full regalia.

I set down my reel of wire and sighed. *These costume freaks are all such drama queens. Well, whatever it is, let's not put it off.* "What's up, boss man?" I asked him.

He nodded at Alastair. "Give us the room for a moment." Alaistair inclined his head and disappeared out the side door.

Ghostwalker turned to me. "Alastair tells me the work is completed. He has nothing but high praise for you. I appreciate that. You have done well. If anything, your reputation is understated."

"Well, thanks." I cocked an eyebrow at him. "So shall we settle up? Ten grand was the agreement."

Ghostwalker gave me a slow nod. "There has been some discussion about that. Alastair has persuaded me that I owe you something for your labor. Here is one thousand in cash." He held out an envelope.

I ignored it and glared at him. "And the rest?"

He was smirking behind that full face mask, I could *feel* it. "The rest is, shall we say, barter. Favors."

"Favors?" I could feel the bristling edge in my voice and didn't care. I *knew* the sonofabitch would try and weasel.

"First, we keep it between us that you helped a crimefighter. That would be deadly in your profession. Especially once I let it be known that Doctor Fixit is Ernie Voskovec. Married to Debra. Lives in the suburbs in a tan split-level two-bedroom." A dry little chuckle. "I think keeping that information to myself is more than worth the difference in payment, don't you? Did you really think I wouldn't find out who you really are? I knew before I ever hired you. I make it my business to know everything about the people who work for me, Voskovec. *Everything.*"

I said two words. The first one I wouldn't repeat in front of a lady. The second was *you*. I added, "All right, you got all the cards. But don't kid yourself. You're no hero. Scrape the paint off, you're just like every other rich bastard I ever met. A pushy no-talent making it on the backs of people way better than you, just because you got money and they don't. Your boy Al is worth ten of you."

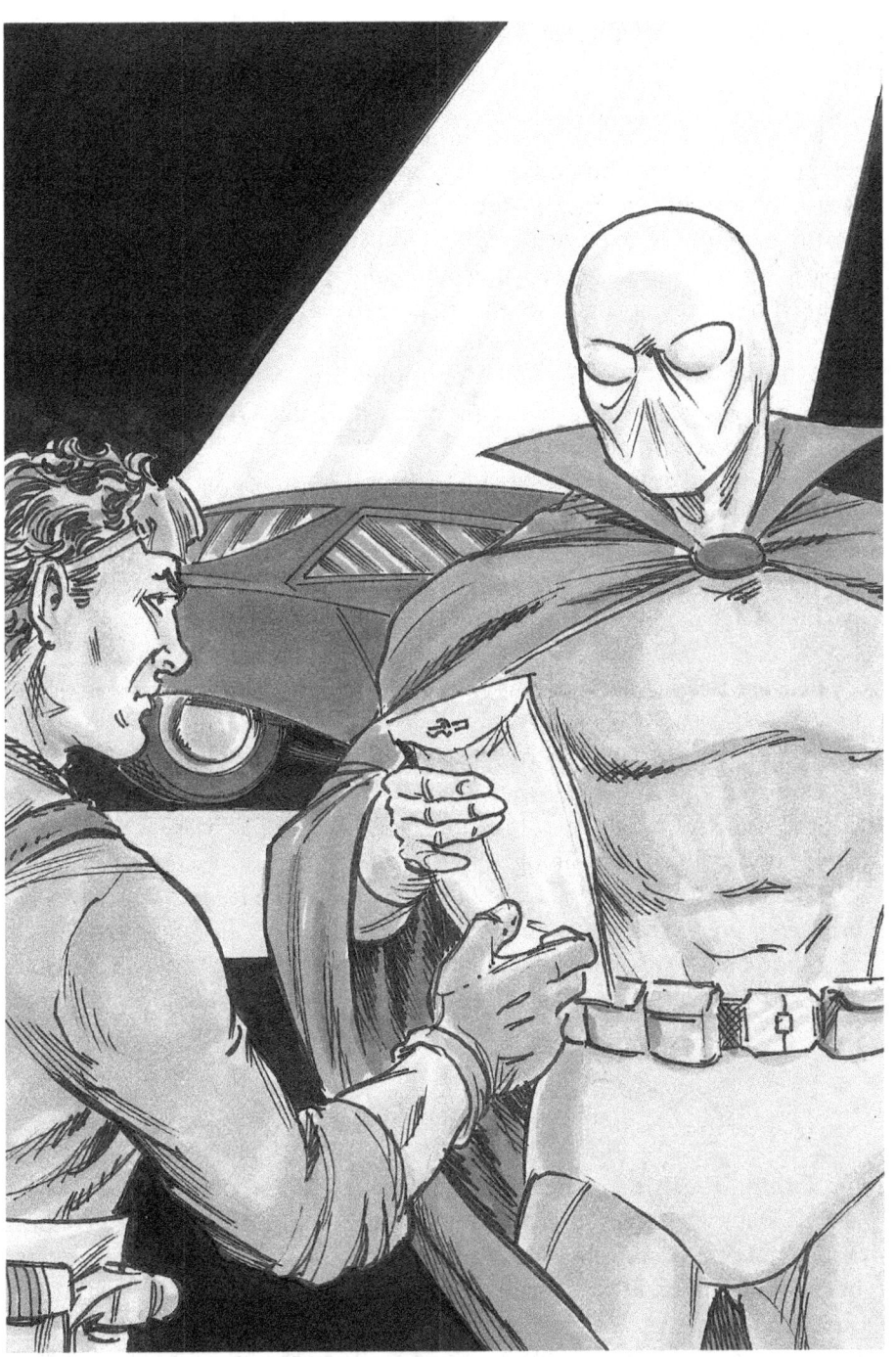

*He was smirking behind that full face mask, I could **feel** it.*

That got to him. The voice hardened. "Watch yourself, Voskovec. You might talk yourself out of even this courtesy payment. Remember your wife."

My wife was the only reason I didn't whip out one of a dozen disguised weapons in my tool belt and let him have it. This bastard would get what was coming to him, but on *my* terms, after I'd made sure there wouldn't be nothing coming back on Debbie. Remember, I'd been at this a while, so it wasn't exactly a surprise the smug sonofabitch would try to welch on me. Hell, I'd told Trav as much when he came to me about the approach. But with Debbie at risk, I had to play it careful.

Still, I couldn't keep the anger out of my voice. "All right. You win. Is that what you want to hear? You got me by the balls. We both know it. Just quit gloating and let me out of here."

Some signal must have passed, because Alastair was suddenly back again. Neither one of us said anything. He motioned for me to follow him and I started to, but Ghostwalker made a noise that might have been clearing his throat and might have been a chuckle. "Voskovec? Don't forget your payment." He held out the envelope.

I took it. "You bet your spooky gray ass I won't forget this," I said.

Because now it was war. Bad enough he'd been screwing over Tina, but now Debbie was in his sights too. That made it personal. Hero or not, I made up my mind this bastard was going down. Hard.

One small consolation: when I got back to my car where I'd left it at Longmeadows, I took a minute to look at the envelope. There was actually twelve hundred in there, along with a note:

I added a little. It seemed like I owed you. I apologize for this. It wasn't my idea. I argued for payment in full. –A.

I shook my head. No matter what side of the street a guy was on, hero or villain, the bosses were jerks and the help tried their best to clean up after 'em. Some things were just universal, I guess.

◉◉◉

Nothing much happened for the next few days. Debbie and I were agreed that the girls could stay with us as long as they needed, and a couple of bugs I left at Tina's place showed me that Ghostwalker was leaving her be. As far as I could tell, he hadn't put it together that we knew each other. That suited me fine. Tina told me that the heist at Reichenbach wasn't supposed to go down for another week or so. The scheduling on it was very tight, she said, which suggested to me that whatever she was supposed to lift from there hadn't arrived yet.

That was okay by me, because it bought us a few days. I spent some time talking over possible plans with Tina, and more time talking to Trav about things he might have heard through his various contacts... and of course I was in my garage workshop a lot, putting together some things I thought would be useful. Meanwhile, my wife was in heaven entertaining Tina and Sarah, and she was even getting some color back. If it hadn't been for the threat of Ghostwalker hanging over everything it would have been almost like a fun family vacation or something.

After four days I was ready to put what I called Operation Payday into action. Tina had her part down, and I had checked in with Trav and made a couple of calls. All that was left was to pull the trigger on it.

"Tomorrow morning," I told Tina, and handed her the widget I'd been working on. "Hook it to your belt and leave it there. If it's not touching you somewhere it won't work. Leave the rest of it to me." I raised an eyebrow. "Sure you're up for this?"

Tina's eyes were hard. She nodded once. "More than you would ever believe." Normally you would never connect nice little Tina Jankewicz with Serpentina, but when she got that expression you could tell.

"Okay. Tomorrow, then. The old outfit's not too tight on you, is it?"

That got a big laugh. "You watch and see, old man. I've still got the moves."

⊙⊙⊙

The Dain Pharmaceuticals corporate headquarters was in midtown, one of the new steel-and-glass monstrosities that had been sprouting in St. Jacques like mushrooms the last five years or so. I went in the main lobby, wearing my work coverall and gloves, with the goggles loose around my neck. I hadn't bothered with the tool belt; the stuff I would need was small enough to fit in my pocket.

Spoofing the executive elevator was easy enough with my bypass magnet—well, that's what I called it, little thing shaped kinda like a tuning fork, we can skip the *Popular Mechanics* lecture on how it worked. I hit the button for the penthouse level and when the doors whooshed open, there was a huge reception area with a little blue-haired lady in butterfly horn-rims sitting behind a big desk with half a dozen phones scattered across the top. She blinked in confusion. "How did you—there's no appointment in my book..."

"He'll see me," I said, and breezed in past her through the double doors.

I thought the blue-haired lady's desk in the reception area was big but the one Christopher Dain was sitting behind was twice its size, a glass-topped mahogany monster with enough surface area to serve as a helicopter pad. Dain was sitting and scowling at a file folder. Behind him was a floor-to-ceiling window that gave him the whole city as a backdrop. He looked up at me and his eyes widened in shock. He sputtered a little, but no words came out.

"Hey there, spookshow," I said.

For a second it looked like he might try and bluff it out, but then he just shrugged. "Voskovec." His voice was quiet and controlled but his face wore an expression of murderous anger. I think it was only the open doors behind me and the presence of the receptionist that kept him from trying to kill me with his bare hands. Instead he stood up slowly and walked around me to close the office doors. Then he returned to his desk and sat, glaring. Finally he said, "How did you find me? We took every precaution…"

"You keep making the same mistake." I shook my head. "I'm not some punk robber you gassed with fear juice. I'm a pro. I've been working with seriously scary people for years. You took precautions? I took precautions too. Took me a little while to work out millionaire industrialist Chris Dain was the big bad boo boy, but I had it figured a couple weeks ago." I pulled a little silver disk out of my pocket. "First night I was here, I put one just like this on the bottom of your phone downstairs—you know, the basement headquarters you have under this building where we been working the last few weeks. It scrambles any call I might make, it's rigged to recognize the particular frequency of my voice, but it's also got a record-and-transmit function. Gave me access to your whole network here."

"But we sweep for bugs! Every day!"

I rolled my eyes. "I keep telling you but you don't listen. This is my business, it's my *job* to outthink hero types like you. The guys what ask me to bug a place, they don't want the bug found. I originally whipped this up for Devilhound, it only transmits twice a day in a coded burst, maybe thirty seconds total. If you ain't doing your sweep during the minute or so it's active, the rest of the time it's just a tiny hunk of dead metal, no transmission to detect. Just a little voice-activated recorder. The only hard part's making it small enough to hide. Nobody on this side of the pond has it but the Russkies been using one like it for a couple of years now. Surprised your KGB buddies didn't supply you. But I guess they were holding out till you actually infiltrated the Liberty Brigade."

That rocked him, hard. I knew it would.

For a minute he was silent. Then he said slowly, "You didn't get that from a phone bug."

"No. I got it from using the smarts and the experience you hired me for. That fear gas gimmick you use, that couldn't have been Alistair. He built the delivery system, the thing in the gloves, but he's not a chemist. So it came from somewhere else. He probably thought the nerve agent was something one of your pharmaceutical employees here stumbled across, but he's not plugged in to the black market the bad guys use. I am, though. I tagged it as KGB stuff from the first night. The only question was where it came from." I grinned at him. "Your trouble is you think the villains are the be-all and end-all. You don't realize they all got support staff, brokers, whatever. None of you hero types ever figure out that the villain's crew hardly ever goes to jail because even a first-year public defender knows he can cut a deal for a henchman who spills on his boss, especially if some masked avenger in a leotard just beat the hell out of him and dropped him off at a police station." I spread my hands. "You and all the other caped crusaders don't think of us at all, but we ain't just background extras in some movie you're making in your head about good versus evil. We're a *community*, we talk to each other. All it took was a couple of calls to the right people to find out we had KGB agents in town. One of 'em has a little side hustle selling his secret-agent widgets and other things to the local masked-villain crowd. He's chatty if he thinks you're in the business and might be a new customer. My broker got a lot out of him." I paused. "But that guy's not your supplier. No, you get yours direct from Mother Russia, the KGB recruited you. I wonder how?"

Dain had murder in his eyes again. "What do you want?"

"I want my money and I want you to lay off Tina. Your deal with her is off. Your bosses will have to find out some other way if this thing Reichen-bach's working on for the military is as good as what KGB has in the works. It's over for you."

Dain's laugh held no humor in it at all, just a sneer. "Seriously? What in the world makes you think I would do that? For that matter, don't you realize you'll never leave this building alive? You've overplayed your hand, Voskovec. You and your wife…"

"That's why I decided to you had to go down. Mess with my friends and family, I take that real personal. You shoulda' just paid me."

"You're no threat to me." Dain chuckled. "You were a fool to come here alone."

"Yeah. About that." I pulled the control box out of my pocket and flipped the switch. "I didn't."

On my right, Serpentina flickered into view, and on my left, Gravedigger did the same. I grinned at Dain again. "Like I said back on that first night at the fountain. I been doing lightbending stuff since '58. I even figured out how to beat the shimmer." Then I looked at the kid and said, "Told you I could prove it. He's in with the Commies. Up to his neck."

But the kid wasn't looking at me. He reached up and tore off his mask and stared in bafflement at Dain. "But... good God... Chris, *why?* All the time training—all the work we did on the streets..."

"It's all about the Liberty Brigade," I told him. "Russia's wanted inside that outfit since the war. They want superpeople of their own. That's why your boy here created the Ghostwalker identity. To audition. You, the car, everything, it's all window dressing. He needed to look good enough they would come to *him*, he had to set himself apart from all the other hopefuls in tights what come to this town. That's why he had to muscle Tina here for the Reichenbach blueprint job, so if it went bad Ghostwalker wouldn't be implicated. There was no way he could explain industrial espionage to Liberty Jane and the rest of 'em. That was just a side thing anyway, his KGB handlers saying, 'oh, and while you're in town, you need to get us these cutting-edge tech blueprints,' like asking somebody to pick up a quart of milk on the way home. He didn't dare endanger his real mission, to infiltrate the Liberty Brigade. That's why he suckered you into his costume gig in the first place, the Brigade's got a soft spot for teen sidekicks. Liberty Jane had Torchlight, Sergeant Smasher had Red Eagle, there was others. Nobody'd suspect Ghostwalker of being KGB if he had somebody like you next to him, all bright-eyed and ready to go do some capital-J Justice. Plus it kept you close at hand and loyal to him so when you turn twenty-one he can get his paws on your trust fund. He's playing all the angles. It's what rich assholes do."

"Robbie, don't listen to him. You know me, you know who I am." Dain sounded a little desperate now.

"I thought I did," the kid said. "But I guess I was just a naïve idiot." He looked at me. "But why did Alastair go along with it? I've known him my whole life. He would never..."

"You'd have to ask him," I said. "The spook must have something on him, same way he did Tina and me. That's all this creep knows how to do, find people's vulnerable spots and squeeze. Al wouldn't tell me what it was but he might tell you, especially now we've taken away Dain's leverage." I waved the disk at Dain, whose face was blotchy now with suppressed fury. "You have fifteen minutes to get a certified check for ten grand up here or a burst transmission of everything we've said in this office goes to the Brigade and the FBI." I paused and added, "You know what? Make it fifteen. I had more trouble over collecting from you than I did building the damn car. You can afford a bonus."

"You cheap crook," Dain gritted.

"I'm an *expensive* crook." I shrugged. "Warned you when we met this was going to run you some money."

Serpentina leaned forward. She held up her hand and clenched it into a fist. An eight-inch blade slid out of the wrist gauntlet. "Skip to the end, Chris. Make the call. Pay him. Or I'll slit your throat right here and now."

I could tell she wasn't kidding and I guess Dain could too, because he punched a button on his desk. "Renata, I need you to run down to Accounting and cut a check to Ernest Voskovec. V-O-S-K-O-V-E-C, yes, just like it sounds. Have one of the girls in the pool take it to the bank and have it certified. Put a rush on it. Fifteen minutes." He looked up at us. "Satisfied?"

"Almost," Serpentina cut in before I could say anything. Suddenly she leaped forward and did a tumbling flip across the desk to land right behind Dain, the blade at his throat. "Now that Ernie's been taken care of I want *my* fee," she hissed. "Your blackmailing women into bed is over with. I'm going to cut your manhood off. You're never going to force a woman again. Even that's too good for you."

Damn it. I knew there was more to it with the two of them than Tina told me but I hadn't put it all the way together.

Gravedigger—Robbie—was ashen. "Chris, you didn't...."

"Of course he did," I snapped. "Guys like him think they can do anything. It's why he wouldn't let you go with him when he went after her. But Tina, you can't—he's not worth it—think of Sarah, for Chrissake. You're better than him."

"She's just a whore in a snake suit," Dain snarled. His expression was the kind of savage desperation you see on a cornered animal, which is what he was now.

I guess he figured he had nothing left to lose. And seeing him in civvies, we kinda forgot that he was still, y'know, Ghostwalker. He wasn't just gimmicks, he had training—serious combat training, probably, way more than your usual spandex case. He was KGB now; never mind what he started as.

Anyway, he spun around all of a sudden, chopping away Serpentina's knife hand and then both she and him were moving too fast to follow, a flurry of chops and kicks and such that almost didn't look like fighting, but more like some kind of speeded-up dance routine. Serpentina still had the knife out but Dain suddenly had a blade too, I don't know if it was a letter opener in his desk or if he already had it on him, they were so quick I couldn't see. He had the advantage because of his size; he had a longer reach. Serpentina was holding her own but he was backing her up into the space between the desk and the window, and then she wasn't going to have room to duck and weave and kick like they'd been doing.

But Serpentina knew it too, and she snatched up the desk chair and threw it against the window. The glass shattered. The main patio was a ways off to the left; the penthouse window was just a couple feet from the edge of the roof. She leaped out on to the balcony rail outside. I thought for a second she was going to fall, but Tina hadn't been kidding when she said she still had the moves. "Let's dance, you son of a bitch. See if you can deal with a woman who's not scared of you." She brandished the blade with one hand and beckoned him with the other. "If you're man enough." Then she laughed and jumped off the roof. I thought for a second she was suicidal but then I saw her catch hold of a power line and spin, then she let go and sailed in a high arc up and over to the next building's roof. She was Olympic material, I'm telling you.

Dain was after her in seconds, peeling off his jacket and shirt to reveal the Ghostwalker outfit beneath. A lot of the costume guys did that, wore the outfit under their civilian clothes. Never understood it myself. I'd think you'd get really overheated.

All this takes a long time to tell but it was less than a minute between when Serpentina jumped on the desk and the time the two of them were leaping and backflipping across the rooftops.

"We have to stop them!" Robbie said. "Somebody's going to get killed!"

For a second I was going to say *what the hell d'you expect us to do?* And then I had an idea. "The *car*, kid, did Al finish the installation on the car? Is it ready?"

"I think so, he was having me help him with the wiring…"

"And the doors? He do up the exit like we were gonna do?"

"I don't know… I haven't seen him since…"

"We have to chance it, I guess." I pulled a little radio out of my pocket and thumbed the mic switch. "Atomic batteries to power! Turbines to speed! Hover mode, auto-home this signal, ignition and execute!"

Robbie blinked at me. "You kept one of our radios?"

"Precautions." I grinned at him. "This ain't my first rodeo, kid. You checked out on the car yet?"

Robbie looked a little sheepish. "Chris said there'd be time enough later."

"Figures." I sighed. "I guess I'm driving, then."

"But don't we have to go down to,,," Robbie's question was cut off by a whooshing roar as the cloud-gray Ghostmobile suddenly appeared outside the shattered window, all the hoverjets firing.

The kid gaped at me. "It flies? You and Alaistair built a *flying car?*"

"Been thinking about it for years," I waved at him to follow me. "Natural extension of the hovercraft design. Al did the math and I worked out the turbine stuff. Between us we figured out a way for us to actually get this thing in the air. But it's not very maneuverable up here and it maxes out the batteries, we gotta move quick. I don't know how much charge it's got. We might only have a few minutes." I hit the button on the radio to open the roof hatch and tried not to think about what would happen if I missed a step. It was a long way down.

When I was behind the wheel I felt better. After the kid was safe in the passenger seat I closed the hatch. A bunch of screens came alive. I said, "Auto-home Ghostwalker, execute," and we were off. So far everything was working like it was supposed to. I'd have been feeling smug if I wasn't so worried about Tina. As it was I was just trying to figure out some way for all of us to get out of this alive. Damn headstrong girl, she was going to blow everything.

We caught up with them in a minute or so, they'd only made it a couple of blocks. They were still fighting. Ghostwalker had shucked the rest of his civvies and was masked up now, and he and Serpentina were trading blows on the roof of a parking garage, bouncing all over the place. Over and through and around the parked cars like some kind of urban obstacle course. Once again he was using his size advantage to press her toward the edge. If she went over, it was twelve stories down and nothing to grab hold of.

"There's no place to set down," Robbie said. "We're too big..."

"I don't want to set down." I looked at the array of buttons and switches. "Did Al get the cable gun in..."

We were still about thirty yards out from the roof of the garage. Ghostwalker got in a punch that sent Serpentina reeling to the edge of the roof. And he followed it up with a kick that knocked her all the way over.

No time to think. Al had got it done or he hadn't. Nothing was labeled yet but I knew where the button was. I hit it and a harpoon shot out trailing the cable I'd picked up last week, thudding into the side of the parking structure a couple of stories down from the roof. Still falling, Serpentina twisted in mid-air and caught it with one hand, and I backed up slow so the cable'd be taut. She reached up with her other hand and pulled herself up so she was kinda sitting on it.

Ghostwalker wasn't done. He dived off the roof, trying for the cable, but something went wrong. He didn't have his glider-cape-jacket and that might have made the difference. Or he just misjudged it. Tina swore later that she hadn't shook the cable and maybe she didn't, but for whatever reason he missed, falling the rest of the way to the street. Nine stories. He didn't even scream.

I opened the roof hatch. "Get out there and help her, we got maybe five minutes before this place is swarming with cops and ambulances and maybe even Brigade. Now, kid!"

Robbie was in shock, I think, but my barking at him brought him out of it. He nodded and climbed up and out to help Serpentina, who was coming hand-over-hand up the cable to us. She grabbed on to him and both of them plopped into the passenger seat, her on his lap. It was awkward and cramped but it was good enough. I punched another button to release the cable and said, "Auto-home, garage." We sailed up and away.

I looked at the two of them and sighed. "This is going to go bad very fast once they pull that mask off his body. And KGB might have a cleanup crew ready to clear Dain's building of anything implicating them. We don't got time for post-mortems. Kid, you and Al are gonna have to get whatever you need out of the workshop before someone else gets to it. Tina, you get changed and head for home, I think it's safe now. Dain wouldn't have told the Russians about you."

"What about Sarah?" Tina pulled off her hood and looked at me with wide scared eyes. It was all starting to sink in.

"Debbie and I will bring her by in a while." I grinned. "After I pick up my check."

◉◉◉

Ernie Voskovec set the sheaf of papers down and whistled. "Wow. That was... something."

"Is it okay?" Christine couldn't help feeling anxious.

"It's better than okay." Ernie shook his head. "I mean, it's all there like I told you but you made it... it reads like a story. I could never do that."

"I just cleaned it up a little," Christine said, blushing. "I'm glad you like it. I did have questions," she added.

"Sure. Shoot."

"What happened with Alastair?"

Voskovec snorted. "Well, it got hushed up about Dain pretty quick, KGB knew when to cut their losses. Nobody really wanted to go there, not the cops nor the corporate folks on the Dain Pharmaceuticals board. Money's a superpower all its own, you know. And then Liberty Jane got into it, so it all got worked out pretty quick. You probably know Ghostwalker did end up in the Brigade. Was a full member till they broke up in '81 or whenever it was."

"But it was Robbie."

"Yeah." Voskovec grinned. "There's lots of high-minded talk about justice and public service and so on with them hero guys but the truth is, folks what get into the life, they get hooked on it. Robbie didn't want to quit and he talked Al around. After all, they had all the equipment and everything. And Dain had played it close enough to the vest that neither the cops nor the KGB found the underground garage. They operated out of there till the Brigade signed 'em up."

"And Tina?"

Now it was Voskovec who was flushing. "Well, I split my check with her. Seemed only fair. Gave her a fresh start. She and Sarah landed out in Arizona. Tina coached college gymnastics out in Tempe till she retired. Sarah's in grad school, I think. She'd be about your age now. I forget the major, it's archaeology or something like that."

"You split the check with her." Christine raised an eyebrow. "After all that trauma to get it."

"Well, she helped a lot. And after what Dain did to her…"

Christine laughed. "You talk so tough, Ernie, but you have a good heart too. You're just a big softy."

Voskovec was still red, but he grinned at that. He shrugged. "Maybe. But don't let it get out, toots. I got a rep."

THE END

AFTERWORD: CAR TALK

I've always loved Big Science in adventure fiction. Got hooked on stuff like *Jonny Quest* and *Fantastic Four* when I was a kid and that led to Heinlein juveniles like *Have Space Suit Will Travel* and the Bantam Doc Savage paperbacks and, well, it's just always been a thing with me. So it's been a real treat to do my own variation on it with Dr. Fixit, handyman to the supervillain set.

I was telling my wife Julie, "See, Ernie's like Dr. Benton Quest if he'd had to drop out of high school to feed his family or something. Reed Richards, but working class. Played by Ernest Borgnine."

My bride snorted. "Who are you kidding? Ernie is **you.** He hates rich people pushing him around and he loves his wife. He gets into this because he's trying to get her medicine. It's so obvious."

Well, maybe. Your output is derived from your input. God knows we've spent way too much of the last year and a half dealing with insurance and health issues, and I admit it was a little cathartic to get some fictional pay-back against a pharmaceutical executive prone to changing the rules at whim. Plus it was a way to make a point I've been wanting to sneak into a story for years... idealist rich-guy heroes like Bruce Wayne and Richard Wentworth, they couldn't possibly exist. No one gets to be a millionaire without stepping on a few people, not even the inherited-wealth crew. It occurred to me that it would be fun to play with the idea of a gentleman-adventurer costumed hero who genuinely *was* the kind of jerk millionaire we see in real life, trampling underlings and taking credit from working-class employees who actually are doing the real labor.

And that made him the perfect adversary for Doc Fixit, blue-collar genius engineer. As recounted in *Mystery Men (and Women)* volume six, I had originally intended Ernie just as a one-off, but when Cap'n Ron asked for more, I suddenly saw a way to do sequels, and that led to me thinking of various cool things Ernie could build. His era's later than most of Airship 27's new-pulp heroes. Doc Fixit's heyday is the sixties, the Groovy Age: Bond, Batman, and bionics, the pulp adventures *I* grew up on. So of course the coolest vehicle ever, the Batmobile, was a natural springboard idea for a Doc Fixit project. (The 1966 Batmobile, that is, or as we say in our household, "the **real** one." There's a reason my author photo at Amazon is me sitting in that car.) The rest came from that.

There will be more Doc Fixit adventures to come. Each of these seems to lead to the next... Look for *Dr. Fixit's Island Getaway* in the not-too-distant future, the story of how Devilhound 'bought it' out in the South Pacific, and what ***really*** happened in the big showdown there with Cetacean. Further deponent sayeth not.

DR. FIXIT'S ISLAND GETAWAY
By Greg Hatcher

Christine Vance looked at the man in the wheelchair and tapped her pen idly on her notepad. "So what have we got on the agenda for today, Ernie?"

"Mmph." Ernie Voskovec's seamed face twisted in a scowl. "I dunno, kid. Drawing a blank today."

Christine smiled a little. This had become their ritual over the last two months of working on the book about Ernie's years as a contract engineer to the underworld.

She was one of the very few that knew that throughout the fifties and sixties, Ernie Voskovec had designed, and often actually built, most of the gear used by the costumed criminals that periodically menaced the city of St. Jacques. Superweapons, secret lairs, deathtraps: Ernie had done it all. He'd been so good at it that he'd been given the nickname Doc Fixit.

Working as an NPR reporter, Christine had discovered Ernie's true identity while researching a story. Eventually, she had persuaded Ernie that his own story was worth telling and for the last two months, she had spent her weekends at the Harding Manor rest home interviewing Ernie about his career. It was often hard to get him started; though once he was rolling Christine found the chapters practically wrote themselves. He was a natural raconteur. She was using a tape recorder, but out of habit she also took notes.

He usually needed some kind of prompt to get going, though, and Christine supplied one. "Tell me about Devilhound. You've mentioned him in passing a lot, but you never really *talk* about him. You worked for him quite a long time, didn't you?"

"Yeah, I guess. Relatively speaking, anyway. Almost two years, from 1959 to the fall of '61. That's a long time in the business we was in. But he got carried away trying to pull off that big heist at the Treasury Building with the hostages. Liberty Jane and the Brigade landed on him like a ton of bricks, and that was the end of that. They had a running battle on the streets all the way back to Devilhound's hideout, it was a hell of a thing. One of the biggest rumbles the supers ever had. If I'd been in the lair that day I'd probably still be doing time—or dead. By the time the fight was done, there wasn't nothing left of the place but a big hole in the street and a bunch of rubble. Everyone figured Devilhound was a goner. I was just glad I was home with Debbie that day, she was having one of her spells so I called in sick." Ernie grinned at her expression. "What, you didn't think henchmen got sick days? The boss didn't care; I wasn't on the heist crew anyway. I just built stuff. But it was a damn lucky break for me."

Christine shook her head. "It's not that. I just— didn't you once say you were there when Devilhound died?"

"Oh. Yeah. I did. I mean, I was." Ernie looked uncomfortable. "That is— well, the rumble—that wasn't when he actually died. That was a few years later."

Christine leaned forward. This was the moment when the story would come with just a little more coaxing. "Come on, Ernie. Don't tease. What happened?"

"It was in Mexico." Ernie leaned back in his wheelchair and sighed. "It's an ugly story, kid. I ain't proud of it. Nobody came off well that time. Not Devilhound, not Cetacean, and sure not me." He raised an eyebrow. "You sure you want to hear this?"

"Of course I do. You're just stalling now, Ernie. C'mon. Give."

Ernie sighed. "Well. The hell of it was, it wasn't even on a job..."

◎◎◎

...it was supposed to be a *vacation*.

This was around '67, a little while before we had to put Debbie in Resthaven. I could see the day was coming, we both could, and I wanted to do something nice for her while I could. I'd just wrapped a job for Ocean Bandit out west—that was another one I got away just in time; a week after I collected my check and left, the Liberty Brigade moved in on him and his crew, there was that big blowup on Lake Mead. I can't prove it or nothing and of course, everybody's dead now anyway, but I always thought it was the mob who tipped the Brigade on that one. Ocean Bandit had a bunch of crazy ideas about being the king of the sea and ruling the world and so on, you know, typical villain shit. The Vegas machine didn't want any of them kind of super shenanigans getting in the way of business.

But there I was with a nice fat bank balance and time on my hands. Believe it or not, we'd never taken a real vacation, just days off here and there, and we'd always promised ourselves we'd take a real trip someplace fun when we were able. So I asked Debbie what she wanted to do and my wife just sighs and says, "Someplace with sun and water. I just want to sit and get a tan and look at the ocean."

Well, that sounded good to me. At first, I was thinking about Hawaii but that was really expensive, and I hated to put Debbie on a plane for that long—it's better now but back then you were on a plane for hours from here to there, plus layovers, you couldn't fly direct. That would have been a whole day of going through the pain-in-the-ass routine of special wheelchair boarding and all the rest of it. I was still pretty spry but she was using a walker by then. So then I was thinking about Florida, but Miami gets so crowded—plus there's a lotta crooks there, and I'd been working long enough, I mighta been recognized by somebody else in the trade. I was always real careful to keep Debbie out of all that. Better not to take a chance. And Debbie hated crowds anyways.

Then I thought, *Mexico's got a lot of nice beaches.* The exchange rate was good enough that a dollar'd go twice as far there. Find a nice out-of-the-way place on the coast and sit in the sun and have umbrella drinks and tacos or whatever. Why not?

I called Trav—you know, he was my broker, he handled all my Doc Fixit business—and asked him to look into it for me. Someplace in Mexico on the beach, quiet, easy to get to, off the beaten path, and not too many stairs. Money's noobject but don't be stupid about it. I'm sure he thought it was something nefarious, another lair job or something, but all we wanted was peace and quiet. I shoulda made that clearer to him, it kinda bit me in the ass later, but I wasn't really thinking it through. After all my years doing what I did, I was just in the habit of never telling anybody everything. Need-to-know, like the government spooks say.

Anyway, Trav got back to me a couple'a days later saying he thought he had it all wired. Little fishing village on the Gulf Coast, on the Yucatan Peninsula, right at the southeasternmost corner of Mexico. "Beautiful white sand beaches that go on forever," Trav assured me. "And nobody there but the natives with a few boats and fishing shacks. No real airport to speak of but I know a guy; we can get you a charter from Tampa. A seaplane that'll put you right there in the harbor. And we can get you a guide lined up if you want to fish, there's a couple of little islands a mile or two off the coast, it's perfect."

"Just peace and quiet is plenty, Trav," I assured him.

Now today you'd never recognize it, it's all hotels and bars and tourist stuff, but back in '67 none of the real estate millionaires had figured out how much money was to be made in Cancún. Back then it was just like Trav said, a little sand spit with a few fishermen. The hotel boom didn't really start there till the seventies. Nobody knew about the place. It sounded perfect.

I had my doubts about the charter but it went smooth as could be. I was worried about Debbie not being up to it but she had the best time, she actually really enjoyed being on a seaplane and kept pointing out stuff to me. And the pilot set us down gentle as a feather in the harbor, took us right up to the beach.

We were greeted there by a couple of teenagers with big grins who made it clear they'd be happy to take our bags up for us, for just a small consideration. I was going to pass but Debbie shushed me and said, "Be nice, this is how they feed their families. Don't be such a cheapskate."

She made it clear with sign language that they could each take a suitcase but they would have to share the money. They were very pleased at this and happily fell into step behind us. That was my Debbie, always thinking of everybody else first. She was managing okay with her cane, so I folded up the walker and put the taller of the two kids in charge of it.

The pilot had given us directions to the hotel—well, really, it was more of a boardinghouse. Just a couple of rooms, it was the only two-story place in the village. Just five minutes' walk from the beach, no trouble even for Debbie. She was having one of her good days; anyway, just the trip and being on vacation had kinda energized her. I loved seeing her happy and having fun, there wasn't much of that for her since her body started to quit on her. It was leukemia finally took her, I told you about that already, but there was all kinds of other stuff too. The diabetes was the worst. We'd had a crash course in the last year about diet and insulin and how to be sort of aware of how we had to watch our meal schedule and mind the desserts and so on; Debbie loved pastry and it really hurt to drop the weekly visit to her little bakery where they did the éclairs she liked. But it was just one goddam thing after another with her health, it was pretty much all I thought about those days. I don't really know how to put across what that's like. Debbie used to say it was like you're at war all the time, but with your own body. It feels like betrayal. Like your own self hates you.

Fortunately for us, Trav had managed to get across that Debbie couldn't manage any stairs, and they had put us in a ground-floor suite with a veranda facing the ocean. It wasn't right on the beach, there was a house across the road in between, but it didn't really obstruct our view.

Debbie let out a big sigh and smiled. "It's perfect," she said; and laid a big kiss on me that made the kids giggle. I didn't care. Moments like that—it makes everything worth it. Maybe you'll know someday, you ever find anybody special of your own.

The proprietor of the place was a plump lady name of Hernandez. She didn't have much English, and neither me nor Debbie had *any* Spanish, but we managed. Through an exchange of very basic words and a lot of gesturing she was able to tell us there was a *cantina* a little ways away where we could get something to eat and maybe a cold beer. Debbie just wanted to lie down but when she saw I was ready to stay with her, she scolded me and told me to git. "Stop fussing over me, it's your vacation too. Go get yourself a beer."

If I'd tried to argue she would have got all agitated, and she was so happy I didn't want to ruin it with a spat. Honestly, things had gone so smooth up to that point it put me off my guard. I'd left all my Doc Fixit gear at home in St. Jacques anyway, and this place was so far off the beaten track I'd let myself quit worrying. I hadn't seen any Americans here at all, let alone anybody I knew from the business.

The cantina was a nice little place; kind of shacky, the screen door wasn't hung quite right, but it was clean and doing a fair amount of business. I sat down at the bar and made it clear by pointing at the menu that I wanted a bottle of Dos Equis and a plate of the 'macho nachos,' and the bartender beamed at me like he'd been waiting all day for me to show up.

He hadn't, but someone else had. A cheerful voice came from behind me. "About time you got here. That charter pilot's always late."

I froze. It couldn't be. Not **here** for Chrissake.

I slowly spun on my barstool to see a balding, bespectacled little man with bright blue eyes grinning at me like an excitable leprechaun. Chances are, if anyone paid any attention to him at all, they would have dismissed him as a boring middle-management type, someone about as threatening as a bubble bath. But I knew better, having worked for him for almost two years. He was one of the most dangerous men I'd ever met. Lloyd Hengist.

I was one of maybe half a dozen people who knew that name. Most people only knew him as Devilhound.

◉◉◉

I couldn't help it. My first thought was *Dammit Trav*—even as I realized it was my own fault for not making it extra clear that there was no job involved with this trip.

Hengist was grinning even wider now, pleased with my reaction. "Nobody told you? Good! I told your guy not to spoil the surprise."

I paid Trav to *keep* me from being surprised, damn it. We'd have to have some words about that when I got back to St. Jacques. He was supposed to

"About time you got here. That charter pilot's always late."

scope things out in advance. Still, I guess I could understand why he didn't want to cross Devilhound.

I can see you wondering what it was about him made everybody so nervous, especially considering the other guys I worked for like Ghostwalker or Diamond Brain. Lemme see if I can explain it for you.

Here's what you gotta understand, first of all; it takes a pretty extreme personality to dress up in a funny suit and commit crimes. The ones that do, they're trying to create—well, magicians call it a stage persona, like. It's all about the image. Calculated.

Hengist was weirder than most because he wanted to *believe* his own image. Devilhound was the guy he wanted to be, not bald little Lloyd Hengist. So he wasn't really about getting rich or conquering the world or whatever the rest of the evil super guys wanted. He wanted to be *cool*. Which is to say, feared and respected by all the other supers, good and bad.

I'd been one of the few guys allowed to know his real name and face because I was there at the beginning, I designed the outfit. The mask that changed the contours of his face and gave his eyes that menacing look also had a sound distorter built into it that dropped his voice an octave and gave it a little layer of reverb. The boots had three-inch lifts. The shoulders were padded to give him a look of strength. The death-touch gloves that injected poison. Plus he wanted his lair to be scary, like something out of a movie. He had the lights all tricked out to strobe and disorient folks, he had a death maze two floors high the width of a city block— What? Where'd he get the money? He always had money. I think he started as a trust fund kid. That was part of what made him so dangerous, he had *no* idea of consequences or risks. You see it with rich kids even today, they just got no clue about the ripple effect from stuff they do. They're always insulated. Hengist grew up like that. Put that together with his insane need to show everybody how scary he could be— well, you can maybe see why we all were nervous around him. You just never knew what he'd do— but you could bet it'd be reckless.

I shoulda known he wasn't really dead. Hengist had a knack for always putting the responsibility on somebody else; he didn't give a shit about the dozen guys that got killed in the Treasury heist that sent him underground. He took crazy risks all the time but somehow he never really endangered himself. And then he'd find a way to tell the story afterward that made him look like the hero.

Now, he had his good points. If you were on his team he tried to take care of you, he paid good and on time and never a squeak about cost even if the job went sour. You just had to kind of *manage* him and his pride. You know, like— You must have had a temperamental boss at some point, right? Moody. Devilhound was like that, kind of jumpy, he could turn on a dime. 'Specially when some of his crazier ideas crashed, those were the times everybody knew to get the hell out of the way. But you could reason with him if you were on the inside. That was what I mostly done for him when I was on his crew, kinda talked him down and made the stuff actually work.

Were we friends? Hell, I don't know. I asked myself that question a lot over the years and I just don't have a good answer for that. I don't have many real friends in the first place and I don't think you can be friends with folks you don't trust. And henching, you learn quick about what a risk it is to trust people. Especially the ones you work for; because they'll throw you under the bus in a second just to buy themselves an extra ten minutes of getaway time.

Let's put it this way. I liked Hengist okay, I guess, but that was all, and he always made me a little nervous. So I wasn't exactly overjoyed to see him there in the cantina that day.

"I dunno what Trav told you, but I ain't here to work." I wanted that out there right up front. "I got Debbie here with me, we're on vacation."

Hengist held up a hand. "Hey, that's okay, I'm not really working either. Although there's this thing I'm kinda looking at—"

Here it comes, I thought. That was the way it always went with Devilhound. You're just talking and then before you know it, you were hip-deep in God knows what and damned if you remembered ever agreeing to anything.

"You know Ocean Bandit went down, right? Weren't you doing something for him?"

"Months ago." I shook my head. "Nothing now. Supers took him out, it's all gone."

"But it's not. That's my point." Hengist's eyes glittered. "He was setting up a base here. Out on one of the islands." He waved a hand at the ocean. "That was his main thing; the Nevada operation was just to raise funds. Didn't you know?"

"Bandit wasn't much of a talker." *Not like you,* I didn't add. "My job was always real specific. 'I need this kind of a ship, gimme blueprints.' Not very much hands-on. I assumed he had other guys building the stuff."

"He did," Hengist said. "Down here. And now he's gone in a giant explosion there in the Lake Mead blowout. Nobody ever knew who the guy was;

nobody saw his face, right?" He leaned forward, getting intense. "So how hard is it to step in as the new Ocean Bandit? Headquarters, gear, crew all in place, just show up and take over. Easy as pie, right? With the right approach, that is."

Oh, Christ. No way in hell— I stared at him. "You have to be kidding. You think nobody would notice you aren't the same guy?"

"What? It's a mask and a suit. Ocean Bandit was even more careful about his real name and face than me. And with you on the tech side to back me up—"

I considered it. It did make a kind of sense. In my business, villains came back from being presumed dead all the time—well, not all the time, but it wasn't uncommon. *With the right kind of work on the mask— add a vocoder strip on the neck—it could work.* I couldn't help myself, I was figuring out how to do it just because my brain's wired that way. "How do you know his setup down here is still intact? Wouldn't the crew have heard the Nevada operation blew up?"

"Even if they did, they'd just head for the hills. The lair and the gear would still be intact; they wouldn't waste time trying to pack up." Hengist shrugged, then grinned. "Worst case, we invest in a new crew. That's doable. I got people in Miami. And I bet some of these Mex kids would like a shot at real money. Any way you look at it, crew won't be a problem. All we gotta do is find the place."

"You got any kind of a line on it?"

"Why else would I be here on this sand spit?" Hengist spread his hands. "When I heard your boy Trav was asking around I thought you must be after the same thing. I figured it'd be easier if we joined forces."

"Nope. Strictly coincidence. I'm just here on vacation. I got Debbie with me for Chrissake, you know how I feel about her being around henching jobs."

Hengist shrugged. "Okay. Whatever. But now that you know, what about it? You want in?" He leaned forward. "Like old times."

Damn him, he did make it sound good. "Lemme think on it," I said. "Nothing while Debbie's down here. But maybe I can send her home after a couple of weeks, tell her a job's come up. Something. And we can dig in after you find the place."

"Great!" Hengist was grinning again, wider than ever. "You won't be sorry."

I already was, kinda, but that was how it went with Devilhound. You meant to say no and it always turned into yes. Man had a gift.

"Come out with me on the boat tomorrow," he went on. "I got a guide and he's got one of them big Chris Craft jobs, plenty of room. Bring the wife. It'll be a nice outing for her and we can do a little scouting around. Nothing blatant, just scope out some likely possibilities. Far as the little woman's concerned, it's just a nice boat ride, right? Then come back later for real. Why not?"

Lots of reasons, it turned out, but dumbass me didn't know any better at the time so I said sure.

◉◉◉

It started as a great day, at least. You ever been down to that part of the Gulf? You'd never believe it, but it really is just like you see in the brochures and stuff. White sand, palm trees, blue ocean under an even bluer sky. Paradise.

There was a little dock at the far end of the harbor from where we were staying, too small to really be called a pier but I guess that's technically what it was. It ran out perpendicular to the beach, most of the local fishermen moored there, and it's where we met Hengist the next day, a little before eleven. He'd never met Debbie before, obviously, but he was all smiles and at his most charming. Devilhound could always turn on the charm when he needed to. In a weird way, it was kinda flattering, that he was bringing his A-game just for my Debbie.

"So pleased to meet you at last," Hengist said when I introduced them. "Ernie always said you lit up his world and I can see why."

Debbie blushed and giggled.

I raised an eyebrow at Hengist and he winked at me. "Come on out," he went on. "I've got us a boat and a guide." He stepped out onto the dock and we followed.

The boat was a beautiful forty-foot Chris Craft, a Roamer that could have slept six. Hengist gestured for us to climb aboard and we did. I thought I might have to help Debbie on the ladderway but she was having another good day, and it was only four steps to the deck.

"It's just us," Hengist said. "—and Mickey. Come up and say hello, Mick."

Mickey was a giant Samoan kid, all smiles. He emerged from the cabin below decks and held out a hand I could have sat in. I shook it and gestured at Debbie. "Hey. I'm Ernie and this is my wife Debbie."

He grinned at Debbie and then turned to me. "Nice to meetcha. Drinks? Beer, mebbe?"

I winced. "Too early for me."

"Iced tea, I think, Mick," Hengist said firmly. "All around."

Mickey disappeared below again. I looked around the deck and whistled. "Nice boat," I said. "It's okay for open water?"

"Well, I took it across the Gulf," Hengist said. "From Florida. Smooth as could be. We had really good weather all the way; it wasn't much of a challenge. Bought it in Pensacola. Mickey came with the boat, he was crewing for the previous owner and I just kept him on. He does most of the hard part: navigating, cooking, maintenance. But really, it almost sails itself."

I wondered if Mickey knew about Hengist being Devilhound. He'd almost have to if he was helping Hengist find the Ocean Bandit's base. Then Debbie smiled at me and I reminded myself, *not working, on vacation.* She was still managing with just the cane, which was a good sign.

"You doing okay?" I asked her.

"So far. I'd like to sit down, though." She moved to a bench built into the rear starboard bulkhead, opposite the engine housing.

"Of course, of course." Hengist was suddenly solicitous. "Both of you, please, make yourselves comfortable. Ah, here we go," he added as Mickey emerged with a tray of drinks. Hengist took the tray from him and said, "Let's get underway, Mick."

Mickey nodded and climbed to the upper deck, where there was a covered pilot's seat and the cockpit controls. He turned a key and I felt a deep rumble as the engines fired up. Hengist looked pleased and handed each of us our drinks. Debbie laughed delightedly when she saw they had tiny umbrellas in them.

For a second, just a second, Hengist bristled. "Something funny?"

Bless her, Debbie was oblivious. "Ernie promised me a vacation in the sun where we would get umbrella drinks," she said, still giggling. "And here we are!"

"Ah." Hengist was all smiles and charm again. "Well, it's good to keep one's promises, isn't it, Ernie?"

The way he said it sounded a little off to me but I couldn't get into anything with him considering Debbie was right there. So I just smiled back and nodded.

Mickey bounced down from the pilot chair and had the lines cleared before I hardly even realized it. He was quick and efficient and I could see why Hengist kept him on. Then he was back up on the flybridge behind the wheel again, and in what felt like no time at all we were heading out across the bay.

"Out toward the islands, Mick," Hengist hollered over the engines.

Mickey gave him a thumbs-up and we swerved north, parallel to the beach. Debbie was grinning ear-to-ear. She gave my hand a squeeze and mouthed silently at me, *I love this!*

I gave her hand a gentle squeeze in return and told myself I should unbend a little. It seemed like Hengist was on the level. *Just enjoy the day. You keep telling everybody you're on vacation. Act like it.*

"The fishing is amazing out by where we're headed," Hengist bellowed. He winked at me again as if to say, *See? I'm not giving anything away to your missus.*

I smiled briefly at him and shook my head. "Just happy to see the sights," I hollered back. "No need to break out the fishing gear on our account."

Mickey was taking us in a long slow arc past the north jetty of the harbor. The water was like blue glass and the big Samoan held the Roamer steady as a train on rails. For the first time since arriving in Cancún, I let myself just relax and enjoy the moment, which is to say enjoying watching my wife enjoy the moment. I'd been worried about Debbie getting seasick but she was happy as could be. We didn't get many moments like that, those days. Most of the time it was just doctors and tests and bad news.

Which is why we're on vacation, I reminded myself. This was why we'd come to Mexico, after all. I was starting to think that maybe I was getting all tensed up over nothing. That we really were just going to have a nice day on the water and maybe dinner with Hengist after. Y'know, like normal people did when they went on vacation.

Then it all went to hell.

Suddenly Debbie gripped my hand. Hard. "Ernie— I feel so sick—"

She slumped across me and I felt my heart skip. "What's wrong? Talk to me, baby—"

But she was out cold. Her drink slid out of her hands to the deck, but thankfully the glass didn't break. I held her close, trying to keep her from sliding off the bench. "Hengist! Get this thing turned around, Debbie's sick."

"Could just be too much sun," Hengist said hopefully. "Maybe we could put her in the stateroom below—"

"No! Back to shore! Now, damn it!" I could have belted him. Of course, he wanted to preserve his agenda, whatever it was. But I wasn't having it, not when Debbie might be in danger. "Don't you dare—"

Hengist shook his head, suddenly terrified. He pointed to something off the port bow. Then he stumbled into me and my own drink went flying before I'd even had a sip.

"For God's sake, Lloyd! Get it together. We need to head back—" I looked to where he was pointing, mystified. All I saw was some weird splashing foam. Like the crest of a wave, but flatter, almost level with the water. Approaching us.

And then I felt it. My head was pulsing with— not pain, not exactly, but it wasn't good. It was some kinda pressure, like. It was— I don't know if I can explain, really. A bad feeling, the kind you get when you know something scary is going to happen, and you can't stop it. The last second before your car crashes. Like that. But it stretched on and on. The unease felt like a physical thing, it was hard to breathe.

The foaming white on the water was all around the Roamer now, and close enough that I could see what it was. Sharks. And barracuda. Dozens of them, converging on us. Like a flotilla of boats in formation.

"Mickey!" Hengist roared. "Go through them! Get us out of here!"

Instead, Mickey throttled back, bringing us to a halt in the middle of the school of predators that now surrounded the Roamer. The shark and barracuda were thrashing in the water all around the boat and I swear I could *feel* them hating us, it was a palpable thing.

Then a human form came hurtling out of the water to land on the bow of the cruiser. A man with long black hair pulled back into a ponytail, wearing what looked like a wetsuit, but with scales. Seafoam green with yellow piping. His skin was pale with a bluish tinge, and his eyes had glittering turquoise irises that seemed to glow. He put his hands on his hips and glared.

"I warned you about staying clear of these waters," he said. "Your island friends have already paid the price. Now it's your turn."

I had never seen him in person but I knew him from the magazine pictures. One of the supers. Cetacean. And he was about to throw down with Devilhound—with me and Debbie caught smack in the middle.

◉◉◉

For a moment we were all paralyzed. I glanced around the deck but it was just a boat, Hengist hadn't rigged it special or anything. Nothing that could be used as a weapon, not even a fish billy.

I tried to remember what the word was on Cetacean. Kind of a rogue operator, enough of a good guy that the Liberty Brigade let him alone but they weren't pals or nothing. He wasn't a Liberty Formula super, but some kind of mutant, originally from the Bikini Islands—you know, where they ran all them nuclear bomb tests. He had a real burr in his saddle over the U.S. Navy because of that, he was suspicious of all Americans. I tried to think of what his abilities were and how to short-circuit them. Enhanced

Then a human form came hurtling out of the water...

strength and endurance. Could live underwater indefinitely. Gills? Mutated lungs? Not sure. Nothing visible, but the wetsuit covered a lot— He'd need slits or something in it though, if there were gills on his chest or back, and I didn't see anything. If I'd been designing gear to take him out I'd probably figure on some kind of heat beam, dehydrate him. Or maybe some kind of chemical weapon, foul his water-breathing ability. Acrylic foam with a sleep toxin. Of course, I didn't have nothing like that to hand. Damn it all.

What else? Low-level telepath; had to be, it's how he was commanding the shark and barracuda. That was the pressure we were feeling, I realized. The sense of hostility from the fish was a reflection, it was because he was broadcasting that we were to be hated; we were a threat. Was it just broadcasting or could he sense thoughts too? Could he read us along with the sharks? Maybe use that?

I tried to make my brain broadcast scared-civilian thoughts. *Just tourists on a boat, no agenda, deeply frightened.* It wasn't much of a leap because I really was scared shitless for Debbie, she was still passed out and I couldn't bring her around, though she was breathing okay. Was the mutant's telepathic broadcast too much for her? She'd collapsed before anything started, was it because of Cetacean or something else? I tried to think if she'd done her insulin. We'd had breakfast and she'd been okay then. Nothing but the iced tea since, no reason for it to be insulin shock or blood sugar, we hadn't even talked about lunch. But the trouble with diabetes is you never really know, it turns on a dime.

I looked at Hengist. He was, in turn, glaring at Mickey, who was standing motionless on the flybridge. Cetacean was standing on the bow, arms folded, looking back at all of us. He had a small smile playing on his lips. Suddenly, without warning, he launched himself into the air, somehow twisting himself in mid-air to land next to Mickey. Despite the big Samoan kid being at least a foot taller than the mutant, Cetacean grabbed him by the throat, one-handed, and flung him overboard into the foaming mass of shark and barracuda. The kid had time for one gurgling scream before he went under and the foam turned pink.

"That was murder!" I couldn't help myself. Now I was scared and mad both. "What the hell, man? You're supposed to be one of the good guys!"

"He was going for a weapon." Cetacean reached under the pilot wheel and pulled out a pistol.

Now I was really furious. "That's a *flare* pistol, you frigging moron," I snapped. "To call for help. In emergencies. Like when some crazy super jumps on your boat and surrounds you with his trained killer sharks."

"Jesus, Ernie," whispered Hengist. "Careful what you—"

I wasn't listening. "He was scared! He was right to be! Who's next, you psycho? Me? My wife? What the hell's the matter with you?"

Cetacean's brow furrowed. "You were joining the others on the island. I know it. I saw this man—" he nodded at Hengist "—circling the bay yesterday. I know how the American navy thinks, I know the men on the island are planning to—"

I cut him off. "You don't know shit!"

It startled him into shutting up. I went on, "You have any idea what it's like for us normals at all? We're not all in some goddam club! We're just people, we're not in your drama! Look at me! Look at my wife here! We're senior goddam citizens, we're not part of some military scheme! You think we're any kind of danger to you? You frigging supers think everything is about you! Sometimes people just go on goddamn vacation!"

Cetacean scowled at me and I felt him probing, his mind fingering at mine like flipping through files in a drawer. There was enough truth in what I'd yelled at him, and the fear and anger I was feeling were sure sincere enough, that I guess I passed. He shook his head. "It is possible you speak the truth. Very well, you may live."

"That's not good enough. My wife needs medical—"

"Do not test me, human." He turned to face Hengist. "You. What are you planning? I can feel you hiding something—"

Hengist just shook his head. "I just don't want to die."

"But you would kill me, as easily as you killed my people in the Pacific islands nine years ago. Even if I couldn't feel your intent I know how Americans are."

I cut in, "You picked this fight, water boy. So far the only killer here is you." I sure to God didn't want him probing Hengist enough to find Devilhound. "Fine. You win. Call off your sharks and we'll go home."

"I think not." Cetacean shook his head. "I don't know about you or the woman, but this one is not to be trusted." He nodded at Hengist. "I think you can join your friends on the island. Understand that my sharks will attack anyone who tries to get away. You want to be there so badly, you can live there." He turned and put a fist through the pilot console, splintering through all the metal and electronics. Then he tore out the whole console and hurled it over the side. The gaping hole where it had been sparked and sputtered. The engines stopped and we were dead in the water.

I stared at him. "What the—"

Cetacean ignored me. He leaped again, this time in a high arc that took him back into the water. A few moments later we were moving.

Hengist started. "How— the engines—"

"He's pushing us." My voice was grim. "What the hell is all this, Lloyd? Did you know—?"

"How can you ask me that?" Hengist looked wounded. "Mickey's dead for Christ's sake! I just—"

"But he's after *you*." I glared. "Specifically. Why? What does he know?"

"Who the hell knows with these super assholes?" Hengist spread his hands. "He's crazy, you have to see that." He looked at Debbie. "Is she all right?"

"I think so. Her breathing is okay. I just wish I could wake her up." I sighed. "What about this island he's talking about? What's there? You think we can find this base?"

"I hope so. You thinking about weapons?" Hengist looked hopeful. "I know how good you are, Doc Fixit can whip up something—"

"I'm thinking they better have an infirmary," I snapped at him. "Right now I gotta help Debbie. Everything else can wait."

"Of course, of course," Hengist said quickly. "But—"

I just shook my head at him and he shut up. I pulled Debbie closer to me and tried to arrange the deck cushions so she'd be comfortable. Her breathing stayed heavy and regular, which was a little bit reassuring. It was like a deep sleep.

We saw the island coming up and then almost in moments we were beached. *So he could swim as fast as a cigarette boat while pushing a forty-foot Chris Craft*, I reflected. Definitely a first-stringer; the number of supers with that kind of power was a pretty short list. Cetacean emerged from the water and glared at us. "My shark and barracuda have an implanted command now," he told us. He pointed out at the water. "Go beyond three hundred yards and they attack."

"You're marooning us here?" I still couldn't quite believe it.

Cetacean smiled and I think that smile was when I decided I would take him down for good when I got the chance. "Would you rather join your friend as chum for the sharks? There is fresh water inland and fruit. You will manage. Find your friends. They should be along soon enough." With that, he turned and took another impossible leap back into the sea.

I stared after him for a second. It had all happened so fast I could hardly believe it. Just twenty minutes ago we'd been on a nice little harbor cruise, feeling like we had the world by the tail. And now this.

Hengist looked hopefully over at me. "Any chance of fixing—?"

"Are you kidding?" I glared at him and waved at the Chris Craft's flybridge—what was left of it. "There's nothing to fix. The console and all its connections are at the bottom of the bay. There's nothing there but a big hole and some torn cable where it used to be. Even if I could somehow get the engine started without setting fire to the fuel lines, the steering wheel and the cables connecting it to the tiller are gone too. We'd have no way to pilot the boat in the direction we want. Tides would push us right back to the beach here, or worse, onto the rocks up that way. And it's too damn big to try and row." I shook my head. "Right now I'm more worried about Debbie. I think we gotta take our chances with getting to that base. Was he right? Were you out here yesterday? Can you find it?"

Hengist licked his lips. He looked nervous all of a sudden. "Maybe. I think I know where we are, which puts the base maybe a half-mile up the beach that way." He pointed. "But it's a sheer cliff up that way. The entrance is submerged and only accessible from the water. I don't know how I'd get in on foot."

I scowled, thinking it through. If I had designed a base built into the cliffs, only way in by water— Well, I wouldn't've, because that would be stupid. "There has to be ventilation," I told him. "Pipes, vents, something. It'd be up top, above, and inland from the cliff. Start there."

"What, alone?" Hengist looked surprised. "But—"

"Are you insane?" I glared at him. "I'm not leaving Debbie. Just go see if there's a way in. Fish boy talked like the crew had been taken out. But if there's anyone up there, bring some help. If we're lucky they'll have a boat with real weapons and we can figure out how to get past his frigging guard sharks and back to the harbor."

At first, Hengist looked like he wanted to argue, but then he thought better of it and nodded. "Okay. Yeah, that makes sense. Okay, Ernie. I'll be back as quick as I can." He turned and disappeared into the jungle foliage.

At least he had the sense to take a route where he wouldn't be visible from the water. I was pretty sure Cetacean was still close by, somewhere, and we didn't need him getting interested in us again.

Then I looked down at Debbie. Her breathing was still okay, thank God. She stirred and moaned a little, but she wasn't waking up. I wished I knew as much about biology as I did about electronics. She was so fragile any-more, and the diabetes turned everything up a notch—or twelve. It was probably too much to hope that the base, wherever it was, had any kind of medic— but maybe they had some kind of— I didn't know what. Stimu-lant, maybe. Something to bring her out of this coma or whatever it was.

I heard rustling from the jungle and turned. Hengist couldn't be back yet, could he?

No such luck. It was three guys in fatigues, carrying rifles. The one in the lead swung his up to cover me. "Don't move, pal. Just tell us who you are and why you're here."

◉◉◉

I tried to think. *Don't oversell it. Keep it simple.* "Fish guy, the super, he wrecked us here. Seemed to think we were hooked up with, I dunno, who-ever you are. Which obviously, we're not." I added, "My wife is real sick. I can't wake her up. Any of you guys got medical training?"

The lead guy was still scowling. Then one of the other two stepped for-ward and put his hand on the rifle barrel, moving it down. "Hey, it's okay. I know him. Ernie, it's me, Rafe. How you doin', man?"

"Rafe? From Vegas?" I blinked. By God, it *was* Rafe. "When did you come out here? I thought—"

"Oh, Bandit wanted the crew all out here; he sent some of us early to set up. I volunteered because I know the coast, I got people out here." Rafe turned to his companions and grinned. "All that cool gear back at the base? That's all Ernie, here, man. He designed all of it. Guy's a miracle worker." He turned back to me. "What brings you out here? You back on the crew?"

"Thinking about it." It was a lie but only kinda. No need to go into it about Devilhound. "Kind of a working vacation. Right now I'm mostly worried about Debbie here, she's sick. I think the fish guy's telepathy might have done, I don't know, something."

"Oh, man." When Rafe said it, it sounded more like *mang* but I'm not going to try and do the accent. "Is that really the missus?" I nodded. "Oh, man. We can rig something, get her back to the base. We got some medical gear."

Music to my ears. I nodded, too grateful for the moment to give any thought to what Devilhound was up to or what we were going to do after. Maybe if I had, it mighta gone different.

◉◉◉

The other two guys were both Mexican too, Luis and Deke. I don't know what Deke was short for. They spoke good English though, and once Rafe vouched for me that was all they needed. They were all three ex-military; I knew Ocean Bandit had a preference for guys who'd been real soldiers. Said it made for better discipline. I dunno about that, but I was glad these guys had some training. They rigged a travois for Debbie out of some awning canvas and a couple of aluminum rails they tore off of the Chris Craft and pretty soon the four of us were carting Debbie down the trail as easy as on a stretcher.

Took us about twenty minutes to get up the trail to the roof entrance. (I *knew* there had to be one.) No sign of Lloyd anywhere, though I was keeping an eye out—not much of one, I admit, because I was working hard just trying to keep up. Rafe and the guys each had at least a decade on me and they were in shape. I wasn't fat, but I was pushing fifty and I wasn't all muscle like these guys were.

We got to the top of the ridge and Rafe grinned at me. "Recognize this?" He tapped the side of a boulder and a little panel slid up, revealing a ten-key button board under a glowing green screen. "Boss adapted it from the one you rigged for Lake Mead." He tapped a sequence and the boulder itself split in half like it was on hinges, revealing an elevator door.

"I'm just glad he sprung for an elevator," I admitted. "I was worried there'd be a ladder or stairs or something."

"No, no." Rafe grinned again. "Bandit goes first class."

If I hadn't been so worried about Debbie I'd'a almost been enjoying myself. It was good to see Rafe again, he'd always been a good kid, and his pleasure at knowing me and showing it off for his buddies was kinda flattering. Like I always said, the supers and the villains were all about the public image and making a big splash, but the rep that counts is the one you have with people you actually work with.

The elevator door slid open and we muscled Debbie in there. It was a tight fit but we managed. A short ride down and the doors opened out onto a balcony overlooking a submarine bay. It was weird because I *recognized* it; I'd originally sketched it on a notepad in a motel in Reno nine years ago. "I'll be damned," I said. "He must have been working on this— What? A decade?"

"About that," said Deke. "I been out here since 1961. He had most of it already back then but we been adding refinements all along."

"Huh." I shook my head. Most of these supervillain guys had the attention span of a mosquito but I had to give Ocean Bandit credit, he'd been playing the long game. Then I noticed something else. "Where is everybody? It's not just you guys, is it?"

Luis shook his head, scowling. "Nah, we got about twenty right now. Skeleton crew till Bandit brings the rest of the guys down from the states. You're right, though, there should be people down there in the docking area and at least one guard up here. Something's wrong." He looked left, then right—and froze. "Hang on." He brought his rifle up. "Body down that way." He gestured for us to stay behind him. "Cover me."

I saw it now, a pair of legs sticking out from around the bend where the balcony angled to go around towards the back of the cave. Luis lowered his head and moved silent as a cat to the body, knelt, then shook his head. "It's Paco. Dead. Been a little while but he's still warm."

Shit. I didn't know if it was Cetacean or Hengist. Coulda been either one. Now I was kinda wishing I'd leveled with the guys about Devilhound. He'd throw me under the bus in a second if the roles were reversed. Rafe turned to me. "Anyone with you on the boat?"

"Local guy, the boat owner." I swallowed and decided to stick with my story. "Cetacean fed him to the sharks."

"Hell." Rafe scowled. "Damn supers. We got defenses but they're all meant for guys who breathe air. He's too small to trip the boat sensors in the entrance. Could have just swum in here and taken out the whole crew."

We moved forward cautiously to join Luis. He pointed at the dead guy. "Not a mark on him." He turned to me. "You said the fish guy is a telepath? Could he have done this? Like, remotely?"

"Possible. I was thinking that's what he did to Debbie." I glanced back to the elevator door, where we'd left her. "Guys, I can't leave her alone like that. Should we go back—?"

Luis was in charge of the patrol, clearly. "No. Rafe, stay with him. Deke, you're with me. We do a simple sweep, clear each area. Call 'em out. Stay sharp. Rafe, anything ain't one of our guys, you fill it full of holes. Specially that fish bastard." He sighed. "Wish the radios worked in here." Of course, we were underground. Never did lick that one, though I'd tried a few times. "We'll use the intercom system. Just 'clear.' No locations. That's for you and me, Deke. Rafe'll just hang here with the doc and keep him and the missus covered. Everybody got it?"

We all nodded.

"All right. Move out."

That left me and Rafe sitting there by the catwalk rail with Debbie. Suddenly I had an idea. "Hey, Rafe. Did the Bandit use *all* the ideas for this place I drew up for him? D'you know?"

"I think so." Rafe's brow furrowed. "What are you thinking?"

"I'm thinking if he used my boat design we might have a way past fish boy and his pet sharks. Did he build the boat?"

"The *Petrel*?" Rafe brightened, then his face fell. "Yeah, man, it's here, but

"You said the fish guy is a telepath? Could he have done this? Like, remotely?"

it won't run. Some kind of battery problem."

"I can handle that," I said, though inwardly I was annoyed. Cheap-assing it and paranoia is always where these villain guys screw everything up. Half the jobs I took involved fixing stuff that had originally been done substandard. Like our current situation. Bandit should have trusted me enough to help him build this place and paid me to do it. But whatever. I always had jobs on offer.

We could hear the guys' voices yelling "Clear!" as they worked their way through the base. In about fifteen minutes they were back, looking grim.

"Everybody's dead," Luis said. He shook his head. "Nothing but bodies. Just dropped in their tracks. No sign of a fight or anything. Nobody pulled the alarm. Whatever it was, there was no warning. Gas maybe."

"I know some nerve agents hit pretty quick, but a place this size, to get everybody—the air would still be fouled." I was thinking out loud. "You guys all are feeling okay?"

Nods all around. Luis looked at me. "And you?"

"Headache," I admitted. "But I think that's left over from Cetacean's attack on the boat. I hate effing telepaths."

Deke was looking spooked. "Who d'you think did it? This guy Cetacean?"

"Not important." Luis shook his head. "The important thing is getting out of here before they come back to mop up."

"Ernie had an idea about that," Rafe put in. "He thinks he can get the *Petrel* to run."

"Rafe said it was a battery problem," I added. "Chances are it's a wiring thing, or maybe just somebody screwed up installing the solar panels. If I can figure out a way to jump-start it and get us out into open ocean, then the solar batteries will have a chance to charge and we're in business."

Luis looked doubtful. "I dunno, no one's ever gotten that thing to run."

"Ernie here can get anything to work," Rafe said. "It's why they call him Doc Fixit."

I appreciated the vote of confidence. I hoped I could live up to it.

There wasn't any kind of real infirmary or anything, so no gurney for us to put Debbie on. But Deke found a cargo dolly cart that would work and even fit in the elevator, so it was pretty easy to get us down to where the *Petrel* was docked.

I gotta admit, even with the fix we was in, it was a little bit of a rush to see that ship actually built. I'd been really proud of that design. It was sleek and scallop-shaped, an amphibious submersible. Capable of going down five hundred feet underwater and also, with the hoverjets, actually flying for short distances. Power was the problem; I'd set it up to be solar, self-sustaining with its own battery system. Whoever Bandit had contracted to build it must have screwed up the lines somehow. But if I could get it to run it was the perfect solution to hop us over Cetacean's shark line.

We got Debbie safely lowered through the hatch so I could keep an eye on her while I was working. She was still breathing okay. All I could do was try and keep her comfortable and hope she'd sleep off whatever this was.

There'd been no sign of Hengist. I figured he must have gotten lost or something. Just as well. He was an added headache we didn't need.

The arms locker on the *Petrel*, I was pleased to see, held four of the recoilless handheld energy blasters I'd originally put together for the Lake Mead fracas, and those were working fine; when I powered one up it lit up with a nice thrum of power. That was reassuring. Whatever had killed the base crew was still out there, after all. I set it down next to me and pulled the housing from the dash to see what was up with the *Petrel's* power feed. Rafe and the guys were outside standing watch while I worked.

Once I had it apart I instantly saw the problem. Whoever Bandit had contracted had screwed up the battery leads: the positive and negative were reversed. Idiots. This is what came of cheap-assing out on the actual construction. It was as predictable as the sunrise. These villain guys never wanted to pay and they thought they were being extra secure by using cut-outs to actually assemble the gear when in reality they were just sabotaging their schemes with their own paranoia. If Bandit had trusted me to build this for him he could have saved all kinds of headaches. Well, whatever. It was fixable, that was the important thing.

The cables were hard-wired into the battery console, which made it difficult. It wasn't like just reversing a couple of plugs. I'd have to cut the cables and then re-splice them to the right leads. About an hour's work. Fortunately, the toolkit on board the *Petrel* had what I needed.

I heard Rafe calling me. "Ernie! We need you up here, man."

I couldn't tell you what put me on the alert. Something in his voice. For whatever reason, I decided to be cautious. My hand curled around the blaster and I moved towards the roof hatch, not the side one we'd been using. Better vantage point.

It was a damn good thing I was careful. I raised the hatch cover as silently as I could and saw Devilhound, in full regalia, holding Rafe in an armlock, death gloves at the ready.

Suddenly a lot of things fell into place for me. I didn't hesitate. I raised the blaster and put a beam right through Devilhound's forehead. It left a hole the size of a golf ball and he dropped like a sack of wheat.

What? Hell yes, I shot him. Listen, kid, I wasn't some hero in a costume, I had no obligation to play fair. I was supervillain crew, henching. I took him out clean and quick and I feel fine about it.

Lemme walk you through it. First of all, he'd been planning to murder us as soon as he knew I was in Cancún. Had to've. He wanted the base, but Devilhound's own pathology would never have let him sub in for Ocean Bandit. He had to be the star. So he would eliminate everyone in the way. He'd been out to the island already and that was probably when he killed the crew. Also must have been when Cetacean got wind of him. No other reason for the mutant to single out one fishing boat in a commercial harbor, or to be so ruthless about it.

Hengist had planned to take me out too, me and Debbie both. Bastard had poisoned the iced tea on the boat, that's what knocked Debbie down so hard. Probably a variation of the fentanyl mix he used in the gloves. But when Cetacean showed up, he'd pretended to stumble and knocked my glass out of my hand because he thought he might need me.

Bottom line was, he'd tried to kill not just me but Debbie. Because of typical supervillain paranoia. He couldn't believe it was just coincidence we were in Cancún. He figured I was after the base too. So he spun a story to get me on his boat where he could take us out, but Cetacean had balled it up for him.

Threatening my wife was a line nobody got to cross. Ever.

So yeah, I shot him. Only time I ever killed a guy outright.

I hollered down to Rafe, "You okay?"

"Yeah." He sounded a little shook. "Thanks, man. You saved my life with that shot. He got Deke and Luis though. It's just us now."

Shit. Well, at least one threat had been eliminated. Now it was just a question of getting us past Cetacean's gauntlet and safely back to the village.

The wiring job wasn't hard, just tedious and time-consuming. Rafe came on board and helped me with it since there was no reason to stand guard anymore. When we were done I replaced the dash housing and muttered, "Please God," and thumbed the ignition.

It fired right up. Rafe grinned at me. "I knew you could do it. Nothing beats Doc Fixit."

"Long ways to go yet." I appreciated Rafe's faith in me but this was just the first step. "Help me get Debbie strapped in." The *Petrel* was a four-seater; I'd figured whoever was piloting it wouldn't be any kind of pro, you couldn't ever make that kind of assumption with villain crew. So I'd been careful to keep it simple and easy. I'd laid it out like a Buick sedan. Standard steering column, viewport in front just like a standard windshield, dash gauges showing speed, depth, and power reserve—we were at about thirty percent—and throttle in the middle between the two front seats.

We got Debbie safely belted in the back seat and then I settled into the pilot's chair. "This could be a rough ride," I told Rafe. "Especially if fish boy decides to make things difficult." I handed him a blaster. "Comes down to that, you take him out."

Rafe nodded, his face grim.

There's really only one way to get ahead of a telepath. You get all emotional: pissed off, scared, whatever. It blocks them from getting a good read on you. I was plenty scared and pissed off already, after our close call with Devilhound. So I concentrated on trying to hang onto that as I eased the throttle forward to take us out. Thankfully the entrance was easy to navigate and in a few minutes, we were in open water. I surfaced and opened her up.

Then we could feel the sickening wave of hate from the shark line. Rafe winced. "What the hell is that?"

"What we gotta hop," I told him. "Hang on! This is where it gets rocky." I hit the hoverjets and throttled forward hard, and we were airborne. The telepathic pressure eased a little as we rose.

Suddenly Cetacean was there in front of us, riding a waterspout. Son of a bitch must have been patrolling. The arrogant bastard held up a hand, like a traffic cop directing us to stop.

"I don't think so, fish sticks," I muttered, and shoved the throttle all the way forward. The *Petrel* leaped straight at him and I was briefly gratified to see the look of shocked surprise on his face when we slammed into him at full speed. For a second he was pasted on the viewport and then he slid off into the ocean below.

Dead or just stunned? I didn't care. We were past him and his pet sharks, that's what mattered. The hoverjets stuttered and I saw we were down to four percent reserve power. We were closing on the harbor. It was going to be tight. I took us back down to the water and we skidded up onto the beach just as the power gauge redlined.

"Goddamn, man," Rafe said.

I grinned at him. "Hey, any landing you can walk away from, right?"

A weak voice came from the back. "Ernie?"

Debbie was finally awake. I spun around in my seat and gathered her in my arms. "You okay, baby?"

"Thirsty," she said. "What kind of crappy charter is this?"

"Never mind," I told her. "We're safe on shore now." Through the view-port, I could see a group of the village kids approaching and I motioned them to come on ahead. We could use the help getting Debbie back up to the hotel. I got her unstrapped while Rafe popped the hatch.

◉◉◉

"So that's the story," Ernie finished. "That's what happened to Devil-hound. Now you know why I don't like talking about it."

Christine nodded. "It's quite a story. I have questions though."

Ernie waved her to go ahead.

"What happened with Cetacean? Did you ever see him again?"

Ernie shook his head. "Cut his losses, I guess. We mighta really hurt him. I don't know. But he didn't bother us anymore. Actually," he added with a grin, "We ended up having a pretty nice vacation after all. Stayed another month getting Debbie back on her feet. Village kids were really sorry to see *Tia* Debbie go. She spoiled 'em all rotten."

"And she never knew."

"Not about Devilhound. Or any of the super stuff. I tried to keep her clear of it. Just that it was a boat ride gone bad, which was true enough."

"What about the *Petrel*?"

"Gave it to Rafe." Ernie smiled. "He had folks in the village. I heard he was using it to run smuggling operations for a while there. Colombian hash, stuff like that. I think the episode on the island cured him of wanting to play with the supers for good. Straight crime was plenty risky enough."

"And no one ever found the base?"

"Nope." Ernie shook his head. "Couple months later one of them big whirly girls came roaring across the Gulf. Storm changed the whole shape of the coastline. Buried it for good. Probably got a resort on top of it now."

Christine shook her head. "I can't quite get my head around it. Just you and your wits, and you took out Devilhound *and* a mutant super? Rafe was right about you. Nobody beats Doc Fixit."

Ernie grinned. "Well—they messed with my Debbie. Like I said, *nobody* gets to do that."

THE END

AFTERWORD:
FLYING SUBS AND FISH GUYS

When I was growing up, there were two vehicles every kid longed to ride in. One was the Batmobile. The other was the Flying Sub from *Voyage to the Bottom of the Sea*.

Since Doc Fixit is a creature of the Groovy Age—when I'm thinking of story possibilities for Ernie they generally are born of my childhood obsessions, the stories from the sixties that got me hooked on pulp adventure to begin with. I'd already put Ernie in the Batmobile, sort of, in the second Doc Fixit story—so it was only natural that my thoughts turned towards putting him in the Flying Sub for the third one, and here it is. With the serial numbers safely filed off, of course. But if you remember the old *Voyage*, I think you can see the line of descent between the FS-1 and the *Petrel*.

There's another *homage* in there as well. There was a wonderful character actor named John Fiedler who was everywhere in the sixties. His specialty was playing mousy annoying little guys who would turn out to be murderously nasty villains. It hit me that he would be perfect for Devilhound, and that's whom I based him on. The name Hengist is shamelessly appropriated from his most famous villain role, the *Star Trek* episode "Wolf in the Fold" where he's a minor bureaucrat that turns out to be the reincarnation of Jack the Ripper.

About the same time I was watching *Voyage* and the adventures of the Seaview, I was also enthralled by the *Superman/Aquaman Hour* on Saturday mornings. In fact, the very first book I ever bought with my own money was *Aquaman: Scourge of the Sea*, a 39-cent Big Little Book from the Village Drug. A pretty big chunk of Grandma's birthday dollar, but definitely worth it; I read it to tatters. Aquaman is still a favorite of mine. My wife Julie and I were first in line for the movie with Jason Momoa not too long ago and my inner child was in heaven—it felt like it was made for eight-year-old me.

So once I was thinking about the Flying Sub, well, it was a pretty easy leap to adding Aquaman to the mix as well; putting the Doc Fixit spin on the idea, of course. The through-line for these stories, sooner or later, always seems to come around to the idea of the supers trampling on the normal folks, and whether said supers identify as good guys or bad guys is largely irrelevant. I've always had a hatred of powerful people pushing around people who can't push back. That's been a red-button issue for me my whole life, and I confess it's been pleasantly cathartic to exact a kind of literary revenge in these tales. Likewise, we've had some medical scares in the last year and I daresay some of that terror found its way in here too. Your output is derived from your input, after all.

But in the end, these things are ancillary; extras that are there if you care to look, but I hope you can enjoy the story on its own merits. In the end, it's just a story, meant to entertain. I hope you enjoyed reading it as much as I did writing it.

◉◉◉

LOOKING FOR DR. FIXIT

By Greg Hatcher & Fred Adams Jr.

Tuesday the seventeenth

Christine Vance kicked her apartment door shut behind her and set her suitcase down. She'd been gone for three days on assignment and was happy to be home. She threw a pile of mail from her box in the foyer onto the coffee table.

Her trip to San Antonio was one of the good ones. Usually, when her boss at NPR sent her out of town it was a quick turnaround and she was back on the plane the same day. On this trip she actually had the time to sightsee a little and sample the city's restaurants and nightlife, especially the Riverwalk.

She wouldn't have even gone, but that stodgy old Arthur Jennings, who was supposed to go, had an attack of kidney stones. Christine's youth and looks were already against her as far as the NPR staff were concerned; no one thought the buxom honey-blonde in her early twenties had the gravitas to be a serious reporter, even on the radio.

Her answering machine blinked six times. Six messages. Probably the office: Are you back yet? Are you back yet? She punched the playback button, dropped into her Barcalounger, and raised the footrest.

The first two messages were mundane; a reminder of her appointment to get her teeth cleaned and a call from the building super about painting the hallway. The third was something else, silence for a few seconds, then a whispered, "It's Ernie. Help me. Get Cap."

Christine sat bolt upright and before she could hit the rewind, she heard a clicking sound, more a tapping. It went on for almost a minute, then the connection was broken. She played the message again. The whispered voice was hard to recognize, but the reference to Cap could only have come from Ernie Voskovec.

Ernie Voskovec…Dr. Fixit, as he had once been known among the St. Jacques City supervillain set. Whatever your metahuman criminal needs might have been; particle beam weapons, flying tanks, personal force fields,

Ernie had been the contractor of choice for any number of colorful costumed rogues that had plagued the city from the fifties to the seventies. Ernie himself retired some twenty years ago in 1968 after the bloody Battle of Easter Sunday that had sent the government super-soldier Captain Dynamo into self-imposed exile and left Ernie himself in a wheelchair.

Christine had tracked down Ernie through a painstaking investigation of police reports of that battle and interviewing the few witnesses left alive. After some initial hesitation, Ernie had been persuaded to collaborate with her on a memoir of his time as Doc Fixit.

That had been almost a year ago. Now the book was almost done and Christine was, she had to admit, getting a little obsessive about the final edits. What had begun as a weekend side project was turning into her primary occupation. She had grown quite fond of Ernie, and she wanted the book to be just right.

She punched in the number of the Pinewood Nursing Home where Ernie jokingly said he was an "inmate."

"Pinewood."

"This is Christine Vance calling. Could you please connect me to Ernie Voskovec's room?"

After a pause and some paper shuffling, the receptionist said, "Mister Voskovec is not here, Miss Vance."

"Where did he go?"

"He was signed out by a Doctor Milovich for treatment at the Rumbaugh Clinic in Shepperdton."

Christine hung up the phone. She'd seen Ernie just a week before she left town, and he didn't mention any leave from Pinewood. The message was no prank. Even after all the years, Ernie still had enemies. He was in trouble and she was the only person he could call for help.

Christine grabbed her purse and went downstairs to hail a cab to midtown. She hoped the person she needed would be available. She didn't want to think about what might happen to Ernie if he wasn't.

What if he won't see me?

•••

The Harding Foundation offices were housed in an unassuming four-story brownstone just off Longmeadows Park. Christine flashed her press credentials as the security guard in the foyer and he spoke a few quiet words into an intercom. Christine couldn't hear the response but it must have been all right because he waved her on through. She went down the hall to the elevator, pausing to consult the directory. *John Fielding CEO, 400. Top floor. Of course.*

The elevator opened onto a large reception area, the centerpiece of which was a large oaken desk in front of a dark wood-paneled wall with a set of double doors. *Old money* thought Christine. *Unusual for a non-profit.*

The desk was occupied by a severe-looking woman in butterfly horn-rims, with steel-gray hair twisted into a bun so tight it looked like it hurt. She regarded Christine with a look of...not disappointment, exactly, but more of a challenge—*prove to me that you matter, young lady.*

I'm the Fourth Estate, Christine reminded herself, and squared her shoulders. She stepped forward with a confidence she did not actually feel and said briskly, "I'm Christine Vance with NPR. I need to speak with Mr. Fielding about a story we're doing on..."

The receptionist cut her off. "Press inquiries have to be routed through the PR office."

"Time is a factor," Christine was determined not to let this harridan stop her when she was so close. "We'd much prefer to get both sides of the story, but we are prepared to go with what we already..."

"It's all right, Vanessa. I'll see her." The double doors opened to reveal a tall, broad-shouldered man in a perfectly-tailored blue serge suit. His silver-white hair was perfectly coiffed, but with no sign of gel or product of any kind—it just seemed to stay naturally in place, falling in a gentle wave across his brow. His voice was deep and sonorous. "Come in, please, Miss Vance. No calls, Vanessa."

She followed him into the office. He gestured her to take a seat in a leather-upholstered chair opposite an oaken desk that dwarfed the receptionist's out front. He moved behind it and sat down, his motions smooth and easy, almost catlike.

Christine had seen him once before, in passing, almost a year ago, at Pinewood. But that encounter had not prepared her for the sheer leonine presence of the man. Everything about him—Christine could not have articulated the specifics of it, but his entire being just seemed—*more.* Even camouflaged as he was in normal business attire, it was obvious that Justin Fielding was a super. Even though she had been researching metahumans for the last year and a half, this was the first one she'd ever actually met and it was a little overwhelming.

They count on that, she thought. *Pull it together. Ernie needs you.* She plunged ahead. "I have a confession, Mr. Fielding. I'm not here on a story, not really.

"Oh?" Fielding raised an eyebrow. "Is it about the book, then?" At Christine's shocked expression, he added, "I keep tabs on Mr. Voskovec, Miss Vance. We finance his care, after all. I'm aware of the work you two have been doing." He smiled. "Honestly, I think you've been good for him. He doesn't think much of me, but I admire him a great deal. In fact, I owe him my life. But you know that." The smile grew wider. "I owe you a debt of gratitude as well, to be honest. It was obvious from your piece on the Battle of Easter Sunday that you must have discovered who I really am, but you chose not to make it public."

"Like I told Ernie, then, it wasn't my story. It's not in the book either, if you were wondering."

"I was, I admit." Fielding looked faintly embarrassed. "I certainly appreciate your discretion. I could weather the exposure but it would greatly hamper the charitable work we do here. Very well, Miss Vance. If it's not NPR or the book, what brings you here? What can Captain Dynamo do for you?"

"It's Ernie. He's in trouble." Christine pulled the cassette out of her purse. "You say you keep tabs on him...did you know he was missing?"

Fielding straightened. "I just check in with the nursing staff once a month or so, it's not as though we have him under surveillance."

"Someone must have." Christine was grim.

Fielding grew somber. "Tell me what's going on, please, Miss Vance."

"It's easier if you hear it for yourself. Do you have a cassette player?"

"Certainly." Fielding pressed a hidden switch under the desk and a section of paneling behind him slid aside to reveal a wall-mounted television and an array of electronic gear, including a small keypad. "Left over from the government service days," he explained. "The Pentagon satellite access is no longer operative, of course, but the hardware is occasionally useful." He snapped the cassette into the slot.

The tape hissed through the speakers and then the whispered words, "It's Ernie. Help me. Get Cap." What followed was the sound of something tapping on the mouthpiece. Fielding frowned.

Christine had already heard the message so this time she watched Fielding's reaction. His expression grew more and more grim as the tape went on. "What is it?" she said.

Fielding held up a hand for silence. He listened to the message to its end. "It's Morse Code." He rewound it and ran it again." This time, he jotted notes on a pad.

When it concluded he turned to face her. "Were you followed here, do you think?'

"I thought of that. No, I don't think so. I changed cabs twice."

"Well done." Fielding's voice held approval. "He hides it well, but Ernie Voskovec is a genius," Fielding mused. "The message is short and very much to the point. If it were anyone but Ernie, it would seem incoherent. You've been in touch with him more recently than I have. Has he shown any signs of dementia?"

Christine shook her head. The last time I visited Ernie, he was as lucid and as quick as ever."

"What about medications? Has he been given something that would alter his mind?"

"Unless something has changed, no. In fact, he complained that the home wouldn't give him 'happy pills.'"

Fielding smiled. "That's Ernie."

"I don't know Morse Code. What does he say?"

"Some of the sound is unclear. Ernie says that he's been abducted and is being held in some sort of bunker, in his words, 'under Happyville.' He says something about Python. Python's been dead for twenty years or more. I know. I killed him myself."

"We'll he's definitely not at Pinewood. I called there and they told me Ernie was signed out by a Doctor Milovich of the Rumbaugh Clinic. I checked. Neither exists."

Fielding frowned. "I see a few possibilities. It could be that someone's settling an old score, or someone wants Ernie's expertise. Maybe some criminal, or maybe terrorists or a foreign government." He paused. "Or ours."

"You don't think the CIA would…"

"Don't be naive, Christine." Fielding stood. "If the powers that be see a need, they fill it in the most expedient way possible."

"What do we do now?"

"I need to put a team together. I think we'd better go see Liberty Jane." He reached down under his desk and another section of paneling slid open, this time revealing a small elevator.

"As civilians?" Christine was taken aback. "Will she even see us? Are you sure you shouldn't…uh, suit up?"

Fielding laughed out loud. "Miss Vance, it's 1989. None of us suit up anymore." He added, "I think you'll enjoy the car, though. Given the situation, it's better to be cautious. It used to be the Dynamobile," he explained. "I daresay it's a vehicle even your friend Ernie would approve of. At any rate, we'll be ready if someone takes an untoward interest. Shall we?"

Christine followed him into the elevator.

The doors opened onto an underground garage. An attendant in a glass booth straightened as he saw them. "Mr. Fielding! There wasn't anything on the schedule, but I can bring the limo up in just a second— "

"It's all right, Jenkins. This is strictly extracurricular. Spur of the moment. We won't be taking the limo today. I'll drive us myself. We'll be needing the sedan. The *custom* sedan," he added.

"Gotcha, boss." Jenkins ducked out of the booth and trotted across the garage. In moments a sleek black sedan came purring up to where they were standing. Jenkins hopped out and gestured for them to get in. "Anything else, sir?"

"Call upstairs and let Vanessa know I'm out for the day." Fielding slid into the driver's seat and waved at Christine to climb in. She nervously climbed into the passenger seat and then they were off.

Fielding glanced over at her with mild amusement. "Go ahead and ask your questions, Miss Vance. I can see you are bursting with them. I'm happy to answer, as long as it stays off record."

Christine swallowed. "Is it really a Lamborghini?"

"Started as one." Fielding chuckled. "Friends of mine at the DOD fitted it out with some extra features. Probably not with the finesse Ernie would have used, but it gets the job done." He sighed. "Of course, I removed the old Dynamo markings. It's just a black sports car on the outside now."

"How can you *afford* this?" The Foundation would have to—"

"It's not the Foundation." Fielding's voice was clipped. "It's my own money. Family inheritance...I would never funnel money through the Harding Foundation for playtoys like this."

Christine considered it. "Family money." She was silent for a moment. "Forgive me, but it seems unlikely that a trust fund baby would...that is..."

"Would dress up in a mask and costume and fight crime?" Fielding snorted. "You're not wrong. My father would have had a stroke if he'd known. My family was the primary reason Cap Dynamo went masked." His voice grew softer, pensive. "It was Amanda," he added finally.

"Amanda Harding?"

"Yes. It was her work with irradiated dihymenidrol that led to Captain Dynamo in the first place."

"And Diamond Brain."

"Yes." A flicker of grief passed across Fielding's face. "Ronald as well. He was a deeply damaged man, but Amanda swore there was good in him."

"Well, she saw a different side of him. He loved her," Christine said.

"That's what Ernie told me, anyway." She paused. "You loved her too. Yes?"

"Everyone did, really. Her heart was so good, so open, it was impossible not to. But it wasn't meant to be. She was…uh…"

"You're blushing, Cap." Now it was Christine's turn to chuckle. "You can say it. Ernie told me. She was gay."

Fielding changed the subject. "I don't think I need to tell you, Christine, that I'm counting on your discretion. What you're about to see and hear has no place in your book."

"Understood."

Tuesday the nineteenth

"They let me back in the wheelchair today, so I guess I checked out all right." Ernie brushed his fingers over a fresh patch of scab on his cheek. "Just some road rash from the chair tipping over." He sat in the solarium of Pinewood Nursing home with Christine Vance and Justin Fielding. "I guess you want to hear the whole story, huh?"

"In detail," Fielding said.

"Okay, gang, here goes…"

•••

Where do I start? I guess that last heart attack. It wasn't as bad as it could have been, but it laid me low. I was confined to bed and a wheelchair until further notice as if the nursing home weren't punishment enough for all my sins.

I've heard it's Hell to get old. More like purgatory here at good old Sunny Dell Acres. Old ain't the issue; it's the falling apart that's the torment, and the thought that I can fix any damned thing on the planet—except myself. But I'm no fool. I don't pay my doctor to ignore him. He says take it easy til further notice, I'll do it. I don't like it, but I'll do it.

Part of my rest cure included a daily stroll—or should I say roll—outside for fresh air and sunshine. Archie the orderly rolls me down the path into the gardens to smell the begonias. They were Debbie's favorite flowers. She planted them right outside the bedroom window. Near the end, she'd hold my hand and just gaze at them for hours.

Anyway, Archie usually rolls me up to the begonia beds then leaves me for a half hour while he has a smoke and chats up the cute young LPNs. I like Archie; he reminds me of me in my misspent youth.

So here I am sitting looking at the begonia beds when I start rolling down the path. I say, "Hey, Archie what's up? The fish ain't bitin' today?" No answer. "Is my sun time up already?" Silence.

A man in a doctor's smock stepped from behind a tree, a hypodermic needle in his hand and a cold smile under his mustache. I've made more than my share of enemies in my life, and I could see where this was headed. I opened my mouth to yell. A hand the size of a hubcap clamped over my face. I felt the jab, and in seconds the flowers started spinning like a ruby pinwheel.

The last thing I saw was a black Lincoln Continental with a landau roof. The back door stood open. The guy running the wheelchair set the brake, lifted me like Raggedy Andy, and laid me on the back seat. My head lolled, a string of drool ran down my cheek, and I was out.

When I woke up, my mouth felt like it was full of sand. I was wearing the same khaki slacks and turtlenecked sweater I had on in the garden. I thought I was back in my room at the nursing home til my head cleared a little and I noticed there were no drapes; no drapes because there was no window in the room. I could see this because my glasses were still hooked on my ears. A soft whisper and a faint breeze on my forehead told me the room had forced air. The place smelled of two things: fresh paint and antiseptic.

I was on my back in a hospital bed just like the one at the home. When I moved my hand to grope for the control to raise myself and get a better look around, something clanked. I was handcuffed to the bedrail.

My first impulse was to raise hell. I opened my mouth to shout and changed my mind. Give it a few minutes, I thought. Figure it out. The What I knew. I'd been snatched and was being held prisoner. The Who had too thick a catalog of candidates to thumb through quickly. The Where was a complete blank, and so was the Why. I turned my wrist to look at my old Longines Heritage Chronograph. Missing in action. So much for When.

Okay. Time to raise hell. I bellowed like a bull. I won't repeat the language I used. It got the desired effect. In less than a minute I heard the snick of the lock and the door swung open. The guy who stood in the doorway filled about ninety-five percent of the opening. Big, ugly, he had a lantern jaw with an underbite like a piranha and a sloping forehead that hung like a shelf over a pair of dark, piggy eyes. He glared at me for a three count and shut the door.

I'm usually pretty good at keeping track of time, but I was still a little bit groggy from the knockout shot. It could have been five minutes, and it could have been ten before the door opened again.

A short man with a slight build stood at the threshold. He looked like a twelve-year-old kid with a fifty-year-old mug. He had deep lines carved around his features that made his face look like a mask. He was wearing a grey mechanic's shopcoat over a tweed three-piece suit, white shirt, and red bow tie.

"Doctor Fixit."

"Not anymore. I'm retired," I said. "I'm just plain old Ernie Voskovec these days." I feigned boredom as if I were snatched out of a wheelchair once a week.

"You're about to experience a career resurrection."

"Maybe you didn't notice, pal, but I'm not exactly in the best of health here." I shook my wrist and the handcuff clattered against the bed rail. "These bracelets aren't really necessary. If I could even climb out of this goddamned bed—and that's a big if—I couldn't walk from here to you. If I could, I'd drag it behind me and come over there and kick your scrawny ass, Mac."

"Apologies for the indignity. Kidnapping you was a regrettable necessity, Mister Voskovec. My employer assumed, correctly, that you wouldn't come along willingly."

"You got that right, Buster."

"Please call me Walter." Then he said something that startled me: "I'm very pleased to meet you, and I'm looking forward to learning from you. I've been an admirer of yours for years. Your exploits are legendary."

"Say what?"

"You were the Leonardo da Vinci of the Underworld. Anything a villain could possibly want, you delivered; weapons, vehicles, technology, things right out of Buck Rogers, or maybe *Weird Tales*." He left out Rube Goldberg. "They weren't gadgets, they were works of art."

I was flabbergasted. This guy was a one-man fan club. I never thought anybody held me in high esteem, except my late loving wife Debbie. Here was a dyed-in-the-wool admirer.

"I've spent years," he rambled on, "researching your work, trying to re-verse engineer devices you created. I had some success, but I realized I could never achieve what you did in the field."

"Here's a question: how did you get hooked up with kidnappers? Send in a resume? Answer a newspaper ad?" I imagined the Help Wanted column: Wanted: Inventor-Fabricator to develop illegal devices for criminal enterprise…

" I'm not exactly in the best of health here, pal"

"I worked for the Pentagon."

For the first time, he made sense in the whole damned conundrum. "And your 'employer' recruited you from weapons development, or some such."

Walter nodded with a touch of confident pride in the gesture. "We studied your work for the Defense Department, what little of it we could find. Pulverizer buckshot that explodes on contact, the Vulcan Key that melts any lock, the flamethrower cane… Once I started working on the team. I was hooked. I knew what I wanted to do for the rest of my life."

I hated to spit on his cigarette, but I was an exception to the rule. The odds were better every day that working for supervillains would make what was left of that life of his a short ride. Time to cut to the chase. "So, Walter, who is this mysterious 'employer' and what does he want?"

Walter looked around the room as if the answer to my question was written on the walls or the ceiling. "I can't say right now, Mister Voskovec. She will reveal herself and her plans when she's ready."

She? Well, that eliminated roughly half of Humanity as to who. But it unpacked a gross of other questions at the same time. "And in the meantime?"

"I'll do my best to see that you're comfortable. Can I get you anything?"

I held up the handcuffed wrist. "For starters, the key or a hacksaw. Are the cuffs really necessary? The door's locked from the outside even if I could walk over there. And, from the looks of it, you have that ogre standing guard, and I couldn't put him on the floor with a sledgehammer. So, how's about it, Walter?"

"Sorry, Mister Voskovec. I have strict orders to keep you cuffed to the bed when you're in this room. Your cleverness is notorious, and I can't afford to let you escape."

"Yeah? Well, I have to go the John, Walter." I put a sneering emphasis on his name. "I hope you have lots of paper. The nursing home served up cabbage rolls for lunch."

He frowned. "I'll have an orderly come in with a bedpan." He left the room and as he locked the door behind him, I shouted, "And give me back my watch!"

I lost round one, but the fight was far from over. Take a breather, I told myself. Think it through. Figure out the five Ws, then start working on a plan.

•••

As promised, within minutes, an orderly in a white smock came in with a bedpan and a white enameled urinal. "Which do you need, sir?"

I just rolled my eyes.

Supper was good, I must admit. Steak, baked potato, green beans, applesauce, and cherry pie a la mode for dessert. The food was individually prepared. After you eat three squares a day in a nursing home for a year or two, the difference between individual prep and institutional cooking is easy detection.

I hesitated for a minute before digging in, but I figured since I wasn't dead already, that there wouldn't be any arsenic in the sugar bowl. Somebody went to a lot of trouble to get me there; she wasn't about to bump me off before I served whatever purpose she had in mind. Maybe later, but not just yet.

I dropped a dessert spoon into the covers, but the orderly, whose name I learned was Rick, counted the silverware like a host with a questionable guest. He didn't leave 'til he found it. Unlike a convict, I wasn't thinking weapon, I was thinking tool. That's okay, I thought. There will be other chances.

What Walter said earlier gave me a clue or two as to why I was grabbed. Walter was a hencher, like I was years ago, working for the wrong side of the law at what private industry called research and development. I had no choice. Debbie was sick and needed doctors and medicine and hospitals. We needed the money, and as is usually the case when you deal with the Underworld, once you're in it, it's hard to get out without a death certificate. Walter's motivation was a whole other animal.

I admit the pay was great, the technical challenges were fun in their own way, and the mortal perils were often a thrill, but Walter's attitude was a kid at Christmas and I was Santa fresh from the chimney. He was stoked just to be here, and my presence iced the cake. It was Class A hero worship, and if I played it right, maybe I could use it to live through this caper.

I waited for a long time for Walter to come back before my old fart fatigue got the best of me. The only person to come into the room was Rick. He turned the lights down, cleared up my supper tray, and emptied the urinal, but without my watch, I didn't know whether it was eight a.m., high noon, or three in the morning. Standard prisoner disorientation tactics.

Rick offered to bring me a sleeping pill, but I said I wouldn't need it. I wanted to be alert, and that included not being groggy when I woke up. He also handed me a call button on a cable plugged into the wall. "In case you need anything overnight, just push the button. I'll be here in a minute. Goodnight, Mister Voskovec."

Alone again. I spent the time 'til I finally fell asleep running one "what if" scenario after another in my head. I knew one thing for sure: the Who had me, Why I didn't know, so it was up to me to be all eyes and ears and figure it out, and once I had that, work on What to do about it. For that, I needed to sleep. So I did.

But in that last hypnogogic moment, that twilight between awake and asleep, I could swear I heard, ever so faint, the tinny music of a carousel.

Rick woke me in what I assumed was morning. He had my heart meds right. They planned on keeping me alive in the short run, and they were sticklers for detail. I guess they had an insider in Sunny Dell Acres on the payroll. Rick also brought in a bedside service cart with towels and a wash-basin of soapy water. He stepped back and let me wash myself, which I appreciated. But when it came to shaving, Rick said he'd do the honors. "Orders," he said, stropping a barber's razor.

Halfway through my shave, Walter came in.

"Hey, Wally, I understand why you don't want me to get my hands on anything sharper than a tennis ball, but how's about an electric shaver so I can shave myself?"

Walter smiled, amused. "Because knowing your potential, you'd probably take it apart and turn it into a wireless telegraph, or a ray gun, or something worse. We're not taking any chances."

Guilty as charged. I laughed. "Actually, I was going to make an electric lockpick, but even if I got the locks open, where would I go once I got out of this room?" Change the subject. "So when do I meet this boss of yours?"

"Soon."

"And when do I get off this lumpy mattress? Much longer and I'll have bedsores."

"Soon. Rick will bring you breakfast. Would you like something to read?"

"Yeah. *The Prisoner of Zenda*."

This time Walter laughed, and he left the room.

He came back a half hour later carrying a tray with a carafe of java and two mugs. "I thought you might like some coffee."

I rasped, "'Waiter, waiter, percolator,'" in my best Ink Spots imitation, which sounded like Bing Crosby with strep throat.

Walter poured each of us a cup. I noticed he brought no cream or sugar. "I know you like it hot, strong, and black. So do I."

I wondered if he knew my favorite whiskey and my shirt size too. "Yeah.

I learned to drink it black from years on jobsites. If you find milk or cream, it probably has tentacles growing out of the carton. And you don't want to chance the sugar bowl. The practical jokers might put anything in it; salt, sand, alum."

Walter laughed. Good. Let him think I think we're pals. I can use that on him later.

The coffee met all three of my criteria. Walter grimaced when he tasted it, but he was determined to emulate me, and he drank it in three gulps and poured himself another cup.

"So, Walter, you said you reverse-engineered some of my inventions. Which ones?"

His eyes glittered. His enthusiasm was genuine. "One was the boomerang rocket. What a remarkable stroke of creative genius! It took weeks for me to replicate the variable gyroscope."

That I could believe. I spent months developing a mechanism that would cycle through one-eighty and reroute a short-range rocket to its launching pad in full thrust. It was like a gun that shot backwards, a suicide weapon I designed for Reverend Nightshade as a last middle finger to enemies or cops who might successfully raid his headquarters. They might get him, but he'd have the last laugh from Hell.

"And you were able to make it work?"

Walter nodded. "On the fourth try. It took a while, but I worked out the gyro system, and it did what I wanted it to."

"What else?"

"The Ring of Fire. That one was a little easier."

A lot of my inventions were commissioned to protect my clients when they were on the move. I designed systems to make cars invulnerable to attackers from either side of the Law. The Ring of Fire was a group of flame throwers that, if your car was rushed by attackers on foot, lowered to near ground level from a car's chassis and blasted chemical flame in all directions, giving your enemies the world's worst hotfoot. It was great for clearing mobs out of your way too. The biggest problem was keeping the weapon from burning the tires.

"Walter, you're obviously a pretty bright guy. What does your boss want that you can't figure out?" I figured that was why I was there. Wally boy was no slouch, but we all have our limits. He had found his early.

He stammered, embarrassed, and I almost felt bad for him til I remembered I was kidnapped and Walter was my jailer. "I, uh, I can't say. You'll have to—"

"Wait til the Boss Lady shows up," I finished for him. The look on his face told me I kicked the monkey square in the nuts. His face turned red, he clammed up, set his cup on the tray, and left me alone with my unanswered question.

I kicked myself a good one. I shouldn't have asked him such a wiseass question. I probably embarrassed him. I decided I'd stroke his ego next time and it would be all the sweeter for him.

But, it did answer part of the Why. Somebody wanted something I'd made in the past and hired Walter to recreate it. He couldn't do it, and the mysterious She nabbed me from the home to do the job.

But why keep Walter on the payroll if he wasn't delivering the goods? I hated to think about it, but to answer that question, all I had to do was look in the mirror. They realized I had the know-how but not the stamina for a big project. Walter would pick my brain and follow through with the donkey work.

I thought about drooling a little, wearing my shoes on my hands — you know — faking senility, but I understood that if I didn't deliver or looked as if I couldn't, I'd be a dead man in a minute. So, like a circus juggler, as long as I kept the balls in the air, I'd keep breathing. Tell Walter just enough, not the whole shmear, just enough to make things look convincing while I worked up a plan to get out of the place.

And I knew I had to escape. When the job was done, they'd pitch me like last week's newspapers. First, to keep me from blowing the whistle on them, and second, to keep my handiwork their exclusive property. If I got the chance, I'd argue the case that I could keep cranking out gadgets if they let me stay alive, but that was iffy at best.

A little later in the morning, Walter came in, and behind him was the ogre with my wheelchair. Walter was a little chilly, like a businessman who dislikes a customer but whose job is dependent on his patronage. He unlocked the cuff from the bedframe, but not my wrist. "Stamper." He waved the ogre over and the big guy rolled the wheelchair to the side of my bed.

"Where am I going?"

"The Boss wants you to see the workshop, to see if it meets with your approval."

That was novel; usually, I had to work in some backroom, garage, or root cellar. All my clients ever worried about was results. They didn't give a good rat's ass about working conditions, and OSHA has no say in the world of Supercrime.

Stamper plucked me out of the bed and dropped me into the wheelchair. Walter clicked the handcuff on its arm. He seemed almost to get some perverse kick out of it, as if to say, "I'm the dumb one, but you're in the shackles."

The motorized Mayview 3000 wheelchair was my own from the nursing home, but it had one minor modification. The passenger controls were moved behind the seat. It could be operated only by a person standing behind it.

The ogre rolled me into the corridor. It stretched at least fifty feet in either direction, cinder block walls occasionally interrupted by a doorway or intersecting hallway. As the chair rolled forward, I did my best to orient myself, paying attention to the number of doorways we passed before turning right or left, and counting Stamper's footsteps as his boot heels clicked on the concrete floor behind me.

I estimated Stamper's height to be six-foot-nine, eighty-one inches, by counting how many courses of concrete blocks it took to reach from the floor to the top of his head. Using the standard formula, I multiplied that times 0.415. Unless my head math was off, that made his walking step around thirty-three inches. Round that up to a yard, and I could calculate how far I was from my room and, I hoped, from a way out.

Twice, we passed someone coming in the opposite direction; one was a guy in a lab coat carrying a clipboard, and the other a man in maintenance greens pushing a tool cart. Neither so much as acknowledged us, like, "Hey, Walter, who's the geezer?"

We turned right, we turned left, we turned left again, and soon came to a steel security door. Walter fumbled in his pocket and fished out a ring with a dozen keys. He opened the door and as Stamper rolled me into the dark room, I paid attention to which pocket Walter used to carry his keyring.

"This is the workshop."

Walter clicked on the lights, and my jaw dropped slightly north of my navel.

The room was a continuous space the size of half a football field. It was my turn to feel like a kid, not on Christmas morning, but on his first visit to Coney Island.

The fabrication area was big enough and sufficiently equipped to build a Sherman tank from scratch, and in a far corner, I saw a foundry where you could cast all the parts. Among other things, the shop featured industrial welders, lathes, a complete tool and die forge to create any necessary tool or part, a chemical lab, a dust-free paint booth, and a winding station to create electric motors and generators. The kicker was a drafting area with overhead projection screens.

I was used to working in abandoned warehouses, basements ankle-deep in water, and even an empty refinery tank once. This was everything I ever dreamed of in a workshop. And then some. I couldn't have designed it better myself.

I could build literally anything in the place.

"So what do you think, Mister Voskovec?"

I suddenly knew how Faustus felt with Mephistopheles whispering in his ear.

I realize now that the dramatic revelation of the dream factory was calculated to soften me up for the big reveal. It took me a few breaths to compose myself enough to say offhandedly, "Looks adequate."

A sibilant voice behind me said, "I'm glad you approve, Missster Vossskovec."

Stamper turned my wheelchair toward the speaker, and my jaw dropped the rest of the way.

I thought I was dreaming or maybe they put magic mushrooms in my orange juice. Standing in front of me was Python. It couldn't be Python, I told myself. He was twenty years dead. I saw it happen. Caped and cowled, the arch-criminal stood in an arrogant pose, crossed arms and raised chin.

But there was the angular face, the hairless head, the hooded eyes, the flat nostrils, and the grey skin with its dime-sized scales, hands, face, and throat. I shook my head like a wet Beagle and looked again. This time I saw something I missed the first gander, curves under that dark cloak that would make Jayne Mansfield proud.

She.

The Boss.

"Twenty-seven million dollars."

I blinked. "Say what?"

"You were estimating the cost of this facility."

"I was guessing twenty-five."

"Things do cost a little more than they once did."

I wanted to make some snappy remark about a larcenous discount, but it just wouldn't come. The scene was designed to overwhelm me, and it was working pretty well.

"You worked for Python in the old days. You were with him when he died."

"Yes."

I was building The Worm, a subterranean burrower with a cutting head that chewed through the earth at its front and passed the dislodged earth behind it with a rotating screw-threaded shell, filling in its trail as it went. The cutters would even gnaw through reinforced concrete like you'd find in the floor of a bank vault or jewelry store, or prison cell.

I was in the cockpit preparing it for a field test when you busted in with a Supercop posse, Cap. Guns were drawn, and I was lucky to not get hit. Python wasn't so lucky. He took two in the chest.

I saw the way things were headed, and I fired up the Worm. In thirty seconds, I had chewed through the floor of the old roundhouse where I was working, and I was on my way. You would have tried to follow me, but you'd have needed a team of sandhogs and a week to clear the tunnel. The Worm went great for almost a mile before the cooling system failed and it started to overheat. I figured I'd better break the surface before the machine conked out and left me buried in a hundred-thousand-dollar coffin.

It popped out of the ground in the middle of St. Jacques' Huddleston Park. I bailed out and ran, but before I did, I tripped the self-destruct switch so the Good Guys wouldn't get the gadget. I'm glad it was three in the morning. Nobody was hurt but the blast took out a half acre of playgrounds and maple groves. I always felt bad about that, but a major plank in my operating credo was to leave nothing the opposition could use.

"So why did you put the grab on me?" Her answer made my blood run cold.

"I want you to work for me, just as you did for my father."

My head spun like a weather vane in a tornado. Who knew Python had a daughter? Hell, I didn't even know he had a mistress. I never asked any of my employers about their personal lives. I figured the less I knew the better.

Lady Python made a dismissive gesture at Walter and Stamper. "Leave." Stamper turned and strolled for the door. Walter hesitated until she told him. "You too."

"Are you sure that'll be safe?" It was obvious to me he wanted to be in on the discussion and was grasping for any excuse to stay, however laughable.

Lady Python's eyes narrowed to slits. She hissed, "I won't sssay it again."

Walter flinched as if he'd been slapped. His face flushed. He backed out the door and closed it behind him.

She walked all the way around me, like an art buyer sizing up a statue. Finally, she pulled up a chair and sat so she could see me face to face.

"You seem surprised," she said. "People can love sinners as easily as saints." The drawn-out esses were getting on my nerves. "And my mother loved my father unconditionally."

Good girls love bad boys, I thought but didn't say it. "You inherited your father's skin condition."

She shook her head. "If I had, it would have been an honor. No, my scales are tattoos." She pulled down the neck of her sweater and showed me scales all the way into her cleavage. I got the notion that it was a hundred percent job. "Let that be a testimony to my devotion to my father and my commitment."

I thought, let that be testimony to your degree of insanity. I cringed inside at the pain that must have been involved, and the obsession that drove her to submit to it. I decided to change the subject. "You spent a pile of cash to set all this up. Not just this—" I swept an arm to take in the whole workshop. "Everything; this whole underground compound. It is underground, right?"

She laughed deep in her throat. "Walter is right. You are a clever man. Keep going."

"Okay, I'm guessing here. You need a piece of tech that Walter can't produce. I'm also guessing it's something I've done before, maybe for your old man. You grabbed me to guide Walter down the path since I can't really do it all by myself anymore. How'm I doing so far?"

"Dead on." Her voice was the same velvet buzz as her old man's. If it wasn't his genetic legacy, Walter did a damned good job on her vocoder. I had to watch myself. Underestimating the poor shlub could be a serious mistake.

"I built a few things for Python. Which one did you have in mind?"

"We'll get to that. First, some questions: One, are you willing to work for me? Two, are you willing to follow my orders explicitly? Three, are you willing to work with Walter?"

I said, "Four, what happens if I say 'no' to questions one, two, or three? You don't have to answer that. I think I know already."

"I'd rather you serve my interests willingly, but fear will do as motivation."

It was my turn to laugh. "Fear? Of what? Death? How much longer do you think I expect to live anyway?"

Lady Python wasn't amused. "Not you. Christine Vance." At the mention of your name, Christine, the big overhead screens in the drafting station flashed on and ran a slideshow: you leaving your apartment building, you hopping the city bus, you at your desk at Public Broadcasting, you doing yoga at the YWCA, you at the Farmer's Market buying tomatoes, and the one that froze my veins, you sleeping in your bed.

It was my turn to be unamused. I wished for one minute to have my legs

"How'm I doing so far?"

work right again so I could stomp that tattooed face into the concrete floor. You can threaten me all day, and I'll laugh, but threaten someone I care about, and all bets are off. It was at that moment that I made up my mind.

I was silent while I counted to ten in my head then said, "Yes, yes, and yes."

I lied.

"Very good. Machiavelli was right, 'It is better to be feared than loved.'"

She left out the most important part of the quote, the third option: "if one cannot be both." She was educated, but she wasn't as smart as she thought she was, leading with steel instead of velvet. So be it.

"So what do want me to do?"

She walked over to a section of the wall near the fabrication station covered by a heavy curtain. At the touch of a button, it lifted away, and for the second time, my jaw dropped. In the alcove behind the drape was the Worm. It was unfinished but unmistakable. The artillery shell body, the corkscrew superstructure, the powerful jackhammer snout, and the cockpit porthole like a cyclopean eye.

"How do you know about the Worm?" I asked. "Python kept it a strict secret, even from most of his own people."

"My father kept a journal. It had drawings and schematics, but they were regrettably incomplete."

"Which is why you need me."

Lady P. nodded slowly. "But it was more than a diary, it was a manifesto. I found it after his death. In it, he outlined his program to build a New America. People thought he was a common thug. He was more. Much, much more. He was a visionary." As she spoke, her voice took on an intensity bordering on religious fervor, and her eyes got a faraway look as if she were watching the future on the far wall of the workshop.

"He imagined an America that is truly free, apart from partisan politics and draconian control, apart from petty prejudice over race, religion, and wealth." Her fingertips brushed her face. "And xenophobia. His robberies weren't simple larceny; they were the means to an end, the source of funding a revolution. I intend to honor that plan."

I never heard a political speech from Python. If he had an agenda past looting bank vaults, he never shared it with the hired help, including me. In her devotion to his vision, Python's daughter was nutty enough to give a fruitcake a close race.

Okay, let the crazy broad think she had me. I'd work for her in the short run. I'd follow her orders, and put up with her lackey for as long as I had to. And while I worked on her project, I'd be setting up the dominoes, and when the time was right, start them tumbling.

"I'll tell Walter you're on board. The two of you will start immediately."

Play the game. Hardball.

"Whoa, sister. What kind of money are we talking?"

She didn't blink. "A hundred thousand to take on the project, and another hundred thousand if you're successful."

"If? Lady, I've made one before. You want it, you'll have it." I decided to push my luck. "And there are a few things I want." Her brow lowered a little.

I thought fast. "I want an easy chair to sit in. I'm sick of lying in that goddamned bed. I want a desk or at least a table for that cell I'm in. Some nights, I don't sleep much. If I'm awake, I like to work. And I want an abacus."

"An abacus? Whatever on earth for? I can give you a state-of-the-art calculator."

"I've been using an abacus forever. Just ask Walter; he knows how I work. I'm slow without one. I realize I can't have my pipe and tobacco from the nursing home, but I want to be able to smoke. I'd prefer a Kaywoodie with a short stem and Pinkussohn's Potpourri tobacco." She nodded. I decided to go for broke. "And I want my watch back."

"I'll have a clock put in your room."

"No dice. My Longines or nothing."

"All right, Mister Voskovec. If it means that much to you. As for the other items, I'll see what I can arrange."

"Call me Doc."

"Call me... Bosss."

I had a reason for everything I asked for. Especially my old Longines Heritage Chronograph. First, I didn't want Lady P. messing with my head and disorienting me time-wise. Second, I needed to keep an eye on my pulse. That last heart attack made me very aware of every beat of my poor old ticker. I didn't want to die before I brought my heel down on Lady Python's head. Finally, under the face of the watch was a little surprise I'd spring when the time was right.

As much as anything, I wanted to let Lady P. know I wasn't going into this job on my knees. I'm no prima donna, but I'm no pushover, either. I'm the best at what I do or damned close to it. I deserve respect, and when I don't get it, I coerce it.

Speaking of respect, Walter got over his bruised ego pretty quickly. I suppose he had to be resilient working for a tyrant like Lady P. She was the type that never left a ledge for the other person to stand on. After supper, he was back, and so was his enthusiasm.

He came in with a leather portfolio under his arm, and my wristwatch in his hand. "Here's your watch, your pipe, and tobacco, Mister Voskovec. I hope you don't mind Prince Albert. Nobody has Pinkussohn's locally."

Oh yeah? Well, that ruled out Saint Jacques as the Where because Newberry's Tobacco Shop on Fifth Street carried it as a regular item, and so would shops in most major cities. I was out in the sticks, which made sense. Building an underground joint like this one would attract snoopers galore in an urban setting, plus you'd have to grease a lot of palms, city planners, zoning boards, building inspectors, all the way up to the Mayor, and that many people can't keep a secret.

The location issue was bad news. The more remote this place was, the tougher time I'd have getting away once I escaped from the Bunker, as I'd come to think of it. And I was determined I'd escape. But, one thing at a time.

I strapped on my chronometer. Quarter to six.

Walter's portfolio was full of design sketches, pages of calculations, and bundles of notes on the Project. I realized that he and Lady P. had both come to think of it with a capital letter. He reached into the folio, and when he did, I pulled his pocket watch out of his vest to look at the time. Quarter to six. I tucked the watch back into the breast pocket of his shop coat.

"Just checking," I told him. Okay. They weren't playing mind games with the clock unless Walter jiggered his watch and mine both. I decided he was a genius but not that subtle. "So, what have you got to show me?"

"This is all the work we've done so far on the Worm. Let me show you..."

And he showed me, all right. Every detail on every scrap of paper. He'd hand me one, and go on at great length about its importance to the Project. Then he'd stand back and fidget like a schoolboy waiting for my response.

I gave approval in dribs and drabs, pumping him up. If I saw an error, I'd say we would have to work on it even though I could correct it in five seconds. I wanted him to think in terms of collaboration, to get him on my side.

Walter did a pretty fair job as far as he got, I have to admit. Many of the problem solutions I saw were just a matter of my experience, like a seasoned mathematician recognizing a quadratic equation in the middle of a group of calculations and using it to provide a quick answer.

Given time, Walter probably could have been successful building the Worm, but Lady P. was an impatient mistress. I could have finished the

Project in ten days, maybe less, using that super workshop, but I needed to make the job look more difficult than it really was to buy me time to plan an escape.

"This is some very good work, Walter. I think we can do it."

We.

Walter's smile was positively beatific. I had him firmly by the ego.

The next morning, Stamper rolled me to the workshop where Walter was waiting in the drafting area. We were going to draw formal schematics and blueprints. That suited me fine. I've never liked being a "pantser"— as in flying by the seat of. I've done it at times when I had to, but I prefer calculation before execution. Some of the things I've built for the bad boys had to work right the first time because there would be no second. You don't do that flying by your ass.

I also met Walter's "team". He didn't introduce them by name. He introduced them by number. I didn't have to memorize who was who. They had their numbers on their coveralls. "This is number three, our master electrician, number four our foundry foreman..." Six of them in all, they were a complete set, one of every specialty. A dream team if ever I saw one.

"Each one is tops in his field," Walter told me. "I recruited them all myself. With them following our orders, we can create anything."

Our. We. Walter was buying into it faster than I expected.

"So, Walter," I said, "How did you get all the talent? I'd guess these guys all were making top dollar at their jobs before. It can't have been the money."

"The Boss can be very persuasive. They all believe in Python's vision. Also, she has promised each a position of prominence in the New Order."

I wondered what the Illuminati and the Bilderbergers would think about that, let alone the Russkis and the Chicoms. "And all men. Why no dames?" I was sure I already knew the answer.

"Herself doesn't want the kind of distractions women would cause."

I bet. Maybe turning herself into a snake woman bothered Lady P.'s sense of femininity more than she let on. She had her pick of the pack here at her beck and call, and no worry about competition.

At least that was one thing I didn't have to fret over. She wouldn't want a crippled geezer like me for a bunk buddy. Her personal flock of admirers might like the kink, but frankly, the thought of cuddling up to her made my skin creep, tattooed scales or no.

We spent the rest of the evening looking over Walter's plans and drawings. I made suggestions and so did team members according to their specialties. I have to hand it to Walter, he did a pretty fair job to that point.

The specialists weren't slouches either. With some adjustments, the Worm could be built from his version of my design.

I saw a few details that my experience could clear up, but I didn't spell them all out at once. I wanted to slow the process to buy me time to plan some action. If I couldn't escape, maybe I could try to signal for help from the outside. If that failed, I could try to sabotage the Project. I figured if it cost me my life in the bargain, no big deal. How much longer would I live anyway? And what kind of life was it? Bottom line: I was determined to see Lady Python fail.

Around midnight she came to visit. I was already cuffed to the bed. "Sorry, Boss," I said, "I'd shake hands, but..." The shackle rattled on the bedframe

She chuckled. "Think of it as a compliment, Doc. I consider you too good at what you do to take a chance on letting you bounce around loossse. Tell me, what do you think of Walter's design?"

"A good start, but I can see why you brought me on board. He might have gotten it right eventually, but you don't want to wait that long. I don't mean to bad mouth Walter, but if you want the job done right, I'll have to supervise every phase and give it all the final okay."

"Are you up to it?"

"I wouldn't miss it for anything," I told her. "I decided I'm going out with a bang, not a whimper."

"How long?"

"Two weeks."

"Ten days." Lady P. stood. "I'll have your abacus here tomorrow. Show me results and I'll see about the easy chair." Her dark violet cloak billowed around her as she swept out of the room. I pushed and she pushed back, standard negotiations. She'd eventually give me what I wanted.

Ten days. Hell, ten years ago with a setup like that I could have made it in a week with time for cocktails at seven. Besides, I didn't plan on hanging around that long.

I had a pipefull of Prince Albert. The tobacco was lousy, but taste wasn't why I wanted to smoke. I was hoping for a lighter, but matches would do. And the aromatic smoke would cover the smell of whatever might be going on. I pushed the call button.

Rick came in. "How may I help you, Mister Voskovec?"

"Been a long day, Rick. I'm sore from being in the wheelchair. Can you bring me a sleeping pill? Otherwise, the pain will keep me up all night."

He came back with a blue tablet and poured me a glass of water. I faked taking it, palmed the pill into my pocket, then lay back, and closed my eyes. "Turn the lights down, Rick. I'm going to sleep."

"Can I get you anything else?"

"No, Rick, thanks. It's been a long day."

"If you do need something, just push the call button."

He left, and I counted to a hundred before I moved. I rolled on my side and slid my hand in the hip pocket of the coveralls they gave me to wear to retrieve the finger-length strip of stainless steel I'd spotted on a workbench in the shop. It was thin and flat, rigid as a D.I.'s backbone, and tapered from a quarter inch at one end to a point at the other. I put the point in a joint between two parts of the bed frame. A silver lining to weak legs, if you can call it that: your hands and arms get a lot stronger. With a little grunt and strain, I bent a short right-angled hook in the steel scrap.

Picking the handcuff lock took fifteen seconds. I timed it on my watch. How long things take is always good to know for next time. Free to move, I reached for the bed control on the washstand. The Healthways motorized adjustable bed was a newer version of the same model in my room in the home. It was state-of-the-art and whisper quiet.

I lowered it as far as it would go. My feet could reach the floor, for all the good they could do me. But I didn't need my legs for that night's recon mission. What I wanted to see was under the bed. I struck a match. There was a wealth of motors, gears, relays, and wiring. What I wanted, I found under the upper end, a junction box labeled Danger with crossed lightning bolts, two hundred twenty volts worth.

I was in luck. The box was covered with a steel plate held by four screws. It took patience, but I got them off. Inside were the standard three wires branching from the junction box to the four servo motors. Okay. Got power. Now, all I needed were a few supplies, and those I'd swipe from the workshop.

I replaced the screws in the box and left them loose enough to unscrew with my fingers. I pulled myself back into the bed. I raised it, and in two minutes, the room looked as if nothing had happened. I opened the seam in the cuff of my coveralls and slid my makeshift lockpick into it. I pulled the covers to my chin and shut my eyes, but my mind was in overdrive.

It was a good thing I got back in bed when I did, because soon after, I heard the snick of the lock, and someone came in to check on me, stayed a few seconds, and left. I kept my eyes shut and breathed steadily. I was glad whoever it was didn't come close, because he might have smelled the sweat on me. I won't lie to you. It was an exertion for me to climb out of that bed and back again.

I won't bore you with the details of the next few days working on the Project. It was twelve or fourteen hours a day and it was exhausting because I insisted on eyeballing every detail. Three things happened of note:

The day after I got a look at my bed, Stamper was rolling me to the workshop when I figured out which way to the exit. I had worked out an orientation system based on the door to my room. To the right, the long corridor just outside was twelve o'clock, to the left, six. I had gone twelve o'clock for sixty feet, nine o'clock for thirty, and six o'clock for almost as far when I felt a blast of cold, damp air from a three o'clock corridor twice as wide as the others. The foundry had a huge exhaust port overhead. Replacement air had to come from someplace. So did supplies. Something told me that was the way out.

Two days later, a foundry worker suffered a bad burn when a crucible spilled hot metal. In the confusion, I grabbed a pair of needle-nosed pliers and some scraps of wire from the table where I was checking the wiring on a control module. Walter rolled me back to my room. I lucked out. In the chaos, nobody counted the spoons.

My biggest problem at the moment was hiding what I stole. I could push the wire into a seam of my coveralls, but the pliers were another story. The wheelchair would be the second place they'd look after the mattress. I was lucky the handles on the pliers were joined at the pivot by a screw and not a rivet. I took them apart and pulled the plastic cap off one of the pipes on the rollaway table. They barely fit which was good. No one would suspect they were hidden in there if they came looking.

There was no camera in my roo, or even a microphone. Otherwise, they would have tumbled to my antics already and stopped the show. I was cooperating with the team and playing the role of the good little Do Bee. I was counting on Lady P.'s obsession to blind her to peril. She believed I was on her side because she needed me, and her ego wouldn't let her believe I didn't share her enthusiasm. That would be her downfall.

The third thing that happened was a failure, with a little help from yours truly. We were working on the command module for the Worm, and Walter was called away for a few minutes to deal with a supply issue. Knowing what I did about the circuitry, I had only to push a piece of wire in the right place.

When Walter returned, we powered it up and resistors popped like firecrackers. Modules that had taken days to assemble burst into flames and the whole works was destroyed in seconds. Walter's face went pale from shock to frustration to terror at Lady P.'s anticipated reaction.

"I don't understand it," he said. "I checked those circuits myself, and so did you."

"We messed up, Walter," I told him. "We'll start again tomorrow."

As he rolled me to my room, I lit my pipe, puffing away and watching the smoke. When we passed the three o'clock corridor. The smoke drifted right. And I heard it again, the faint sound of a carousel. Late in my teens, I spent a year working with a carnival, and nothing on this earth sounds quite like the brittle music of a merry-go-round.

Suddenly I got an idea of where I might be. If I could escape the underground, I'd have half a chance to get away clean. All I needed to figure out now was how to call for the cavalry.

That gear in the works came the next day when Walter wheeled me to the shop. A door opened as we passed by in the twelve o'clock corridor, Number Four, the electrician, stepped out. He left the door open just long enough for me to see a chair, a desk, and on it a telephone.

The rest of that day, I worked on the damaged module with both hands and half of my mind. The handcuff was off when I was in the shop although I was still cuffed to the wheelchair and the bed at night. The other half of my brain was doing five hundred RPMs playing out escape scenarios. I convinced myself that if I played it right, I could not only escape, but I could also bring down Lady P. and thwart her plans. Halfway through the afternoon, she came in and waved away the rest of the team, including Walter. She was wearing a form-fitting wine-colored jumpsuit with a high collar that fanned behind her head like a hood.

"Isss the module repaired?"

I shrugged, "It hasn't been tested, but I'm confident it will work."

"What went wrong?"

"Could have been anything. It may have been a flawed component, or maybe one of those delicate transistors or chips was damaged because it was too close to the soldering iron."

Her eyes bored into my head as if she were watching for my brain to twitch.

"You'll understand if I find this incident suspiciousss."

I didn't flinch. "We're about to test it now. Stick around and watch the show. It oughta work."

Lady P. opened her mouth as if to dress me down for my insolence, but instead said simply, "Sssee that it does." Her icy tone implied: or else. She stepped back and waved Walter over.

The module had twelve circuits. We had tested each separately, and now all were plugged in and ready to run in tandem. Walter hooked up the temporary power supply. I was about to throw the switch when I turned to Lady P. "Would you like to do the honors?"

She glared at me. "It's all yours." She drew a small automatic from her pocket and aimed it at my knee. "Passs or fail."

I patted the arm of the wheelchair. "Shooting me in the knee won't change much."

"But it will hurt like hell." She paused for effect. "Is there anything you want to tell me?" she hissed.

I shook my head. "Nope."

"Run your test."

I shrugged again. I knew the module would work, but Walter wasn't so confident. Sweat stood out on his forehead like rivets on a girder. He figured he'd be second in line to bear the Boss's wrath. He threw the switch. All the LEDs flashed red three times then lit green.

I smiled. "AOK, Boss."

She nodded, turned on her heel and stalked out of the shop.

Walter breathed again.

I was lucky that when Stamper threw me in the car, he threw the nursing home's wheelchair in after me. On boredom days at the home, I tinkered with it and made a few modifications of my own. The Mayview 3000 ran on belts and pulleys, not gears. I worked out the ratios on my abacus and figured that by a little belt swapping, I could get the chair to do twenty miles per hour easy, enough to outrun anybody on foot. I just couldn't outrun a bullet. The battery would drain pretty fast, but I wouldn't be running it very long.

It helped too, that they left the 3000 in the room with me. I guess they figured that with the door locked and me cuffed to the bedrail, the chair wasn't going anywhere.

My next move was to try for the phone in the room down the hall. The doors all had the same kind of knob locks, and I could pick any of them in seconds. I'd have to pull the stunt in the one-digit hours. Rick may have been on call, but he never showed up unbidden after midnight.

I remembered your number, Christine, and I knew I could count on you to get to Cap and rescue me. All I needed was a dial tone—and more luck than I probably deserved, but I remembered the words of Beowulf from my high school English class: Fate often saves an undoomed man when his courage is good.

"Passss or fail?"

The biggest dilemma I faced was that everything I had to do to pull this off had to be done fast and by the numbers, not a second to waste. That meant I had to rehearse it in my head over and over again because I could only do it for real once.

By my count, it was my sixth day on the Project when we were ready to test the rotating superstructure of the Worm, no easy stunt since it weighed roughly as much as a Caterpillar bulldozer. To his credit, Walter figured that one out. We mounted the machine in a jig that held it firmly off the ground, kinda like wrapping your fist around a piece of pipe. The threaded exterior could remain stable while the works inside spun like the drum in a clothes dryer.

The rub with this test was that there was no resistance. Whoever sat in the cockpit would spin with it like the world's worst carnival ride. Lady P. showed up for this event and called for a volunteer. When nobody stepped up, I said, "You babies! For God's sake. Lift me in there. I'll run the damned test."

The team was all for it, but the Boss put up a restraining hand. "No, Doc. You're too necessary to the Project. Who knows what this might do to your heart." Her eyes swept the room. Nobody spoke for a minute, then Walter said, "It was my idea. I'll do it, Boss."

Ahead of the threaded shell, Walter climbed into the cockpit, which resembled the inside of fighter jets I've seen, and the hatch was locked in place. Walter's face looked grim as he gave us a thumbs-up. Lady P. turned to me and nodded. The control was on the dash panel. Walter just had to throw a switch and turn the dial.

I heard the thrum of the motors and the cockpit began to rotate. Slowly at first, then rapidly picking up speed. At maximum efficiency, the hull should rotate at about two hundred RPMs to clear the soil and push the Worm forward while a gyro held the core of the machine, including the cockpit, level. Somehow, Walter gave it four hundred.

The machine worked like a Swiss watch. The cockpit spun for a moment, then slowed to a stop. The hatch opened, and Walter climbed out. I'd heard of people looking green when they were sick, but I'd never seen it before that day. Walter took two staggering steps, fell on his knees, and puked up his lunch.

Lady P. told Stamper, "Take him to his quarters." The ogre slung Walter over his shoulder like an overcoat and strolled away in Lady P.'s wake.

I suddenly had a free hand to work my mischief. I told Number Five, "The rheostat needs adjusted. It has to accelerate smoothly. Lift me in there.

I'll find the problem." The team hesitated. "Well? Am I going to sit here all day pullin' my pud? Let's go."

Like a school of fish all turning in the same direction at once, they suddenly became cooperative. Number Two and Number Four lifted me out of the wheelchair and boosted me into the cockpit. I called for specific tools and they brought them. In ten minutes, I was finished making my adjustments. The Worm would run, but it wouldn't get far.

We would have tested the Worm that night, but Walter wasn't functional. Vertigo's a bitch, and it hits some people harder than others. I offered to work that evening, but Lady P. nixed it. Instead, I got a visit from the guy in the doctor's smock who gave me the mickey.

Turns out he was the real deal. He gave me the most thorough exam I've ever had. Lady P. took no chances. After Walter's collapse, she was making sure I'd be able to finish the job.

"For a man who's had multiple cardiac events, you're in remarkably good health, Mister Voskovec." Playing sick to stall things was out the window. I could fool Walter and Her Majesty, but not the doctor. "Herself has ordered that you be examined nightly, just as a precaution." I groaned. Just what I needed, more face time with the enemy when I could be working on escape.

He left, and when he opened the door, I didn't see Stamper in the corridor. Either Lady P. didn't think I needed guarding anymore, or he was taking a break to take a leak. I hoped it was the former. The Boss was careful almost to the point of paranoia, but she figured if I were cuffed to the bed and couldn't run a fifty-yard dash anyway, Stamper wasn't necessary.

It was time to try for the phone.

Lady P. was right to keep me cuffed to the bed. She was wrong to think the cuffs would keep me there, likewise the lock on the corridor door. I waited until after three to slip out of bed. I used the corny old trick of arranging pillows to look like I was in it.

The wheelchair was across the room charging. It hurt my knees and elbows to scuttle over the tiled floor, but I made it. Someone had done a half-assed job of moving the joystick control module to the back of the seat, attached by a pipe clamp. No imagination. If I were doing the job, I would have mounted it with brackets plus added a kill switch to prevent me from doing what I was about to do.

I unplugged the charging cable and pulled myself into the seat, where I knelt facing backward. I toggled the joystick, and the chair rolled away from the wall.

Picking the door lock was a little trickier than the cuffs, but commercial locks are designed to keep honest people from opening them. It took a minute, but I got it. I took a deep breath and turned the knob.

Praise the Saints. The corridor was empty.

It took a minute to get the hang of steering the 3000 backward, but I got where I was going quickly enough. I put my ear to the door. Silence. In a minute, I had it open and saw the phone, the desk, and Number Six slumped over it snoring beside a bottle of Jack Daniels.

I rolled within reach of the phone, gently lifted the handpiece from the cradle, and put it to my ear. I got a dial tone. I tapped your number, Christine, and got nothing but the dial tone again. I needed to get to an outside line. The most common clearance number was nine. I tried it, and there was a click and a different dial tone. Lady P. was so focused on big picture items, she overlooked the small stuff, and as the saying goes, the Devil is in the details.

I knew you were going out of town, kid. I hoped you either hadn't come back yet or if you did, you were fast asleep. I held my breath. Four rings and your answering machine picked up.

I whispered, "It's Ernie. Help me. Get Cap." That was as much as I dared. I started tapping the mouthpiece with my fingernail, giving a quick sketch of my situation in Morse code. I was praying you'd tumble to it fast.

I hung up and rolled quietly back into the corridor, closing the door behind me. The trip back was quick and uneventful. I was just rolling through the door of my room when I heard footsteps coming. I eased the door shut and rolled the chair back to the charger. Then I held my breath.

In a minute, I heard the snick of a key. The door wasn't locked. I hadn't had time, but whoever was in the hallway assumed it was locked. The door swung inward, and in the rectangle of light from the corridor, I saw a shadow that all but filled it. Stamper. The pillows in the bed fooled him. He closed the door and locked it. I listened hard and barely heard the click of his heels retreat down the hallway.

I got away with it. Back in bed, I counted my blessings and slept like a corpse

The next day, after breakfast, Walter came in, still looking a little rocky. He was almost apologetic over the day before, and I assured him it was no big deal. "We all make sacrifices, Walter. You did your part, you're okay now, and the test was a success. While you were laid up, I adjusted the rheostat on the rotation control, to accelerate more smoothly."

"Getting sick was humiliating."

"Hell," I said. "It probably would've killed me. You took one for the team. You did good, Walter."

He gave a weak smile, grateful for a kind word. I could imagine the dressing down he got from Lady P. and the scorn he endured. "Don't sweat it, Walter. The test was successful. Another day and we'll be ready for a trial run." What I didn't say was that would be the end of it. Lady P. needed me to finish the Worm, but she also needed me to give a report card on Walter. He was good enough to carry on without me. Another day and I became wheel five. I decided it was time to shoot the Moon.

In the shop, it was business as usual. I was amazed that intelligent, educated people could work at a crooked enterprise as if it were an everyday job. Sure, I worked for crooks, but I always had one eye over my shoulder. These guys looked as if they'd break for lunch and go to a Rotary Club meeting. In six days, we'd taken the Worm from barebones superstructure to a working machine. Walter's team behaved as if they'd just changed the spark plugs on a Buick V8.

I solved the heating problem by using oil infused with polychlorinated biphenyl as a heat exchange element. The EPA declared it a hazardous waste material a few years back, but there was still plenty available in old power plant transformers that hadn't been scrapped. The last phase was a complete systems analysis, that would take some time to double and triple-check every circuit, interface, and mechanism.

We were two-thirds through when we called it quits for the night. I was beat from the day's work and the night before, but I had to stay awake. Supper came and went. Rick shut down the lights, and I waited the longest hour of my life.

The Longines said midnight. I picked the lock on my cuffs, lit up my pipe and puffed like a locomotive, filling the room with Prince Albert fumes to cover the smell of my mischief. I slithered under the bed and went to work.

I uncapped the power entry to the servo motors and yanked a wire from the chassis that led to the motor at the foot of the bed. With no knife, I had to strip the insulation from the wire by burning it with matches. The pliers I stole didn't have cutters. That was okay, though. Copper, unlike steel, becomes more brittle as you bend it back and forth. Two minutes and I had the wires I needed.

The job was simple enough. Connect the 220-volt power supply to the shiny steel bedframe. I just had to be careful I didn't zap myself in the process. I wired in the call button cable, giving me an off-on switch for the lightning.

Next was the wheelchair. I undid the clamp and put the joystick where it belonged. The 3000 had a simple snap-on cover over the pulleys that were installed to allow the chair's speed to be adjustable like a variable drill press. I had experimented with my chair at the nursing home before and found that by rerouting the belts, I could get it to go a hell of a lot faster than the manufacturer intended. It was a simple matter, and in a few minutes, I had a one-man hot rod.

What I didn't count on was my get-up-and-go. I'd put in a long day in the shop, and it was hard work getting out of bed and dragging my ancient ass around the room. It was all I could do to pull myself into the seat and run the chair over by the bed. It's a good thing I was easy on the controls, the hopped-up chair shot across the room and nearly hit the wall.

The next part was the worst. I had to be cuffed to the bed when somebody came into the room, or things would look hinky. I needed to insulate myself from the electrical charge. That sent me to the quarter-inch rubber pad over my mattress. With no knife, I had only one way to cut out a sufficient chunk. Thank God I don't wear dentures.

I gnawed at that pad til my jaws got tired then hurt then went numb. I managed a strip of rubber roughly the size of a dollar bill, but I wouldn't be eating pork chops for a week or two. That done, I managed to climb back in bed and raise it to full height.

For about ten minutes, I lay on my back and waited for my head to stop spinning. I used the circular breathing they taught me at the home to slow my pulse and get my anatomy back under control.

One more job. It took some doing, but I got my abacus apart. I filled one pocket of my coverall with beads the size of marbles and slid the rods into another. I wrapped the rubber strip around my wrist and snapped on the cuff.

I took a deep breath. Showtime.

The riskiest part of the whole venture was about to begin. I piled the sheets at the foot of the bed and set them on fire. I flung the frame of my abacus across the room. It bounced off the door and clattered onto the floor. "Aaugh! Aaugh! Help me! Fire! Fire!"

It seemed like forever, but the door swung open and Stamper rushed in with Rick behind him. Stamper grabbed the burning sheets and ripped them from the bed. He tossed them on the floor and dumped my pitcher of ice water on them. I didn't count on two people coming in. I thought fast and clutched my chest. "My heart!"

"I'll call the doc," Rick said, and ran out of the room. I clutched the call button in my hand. Stamper leaned over the bed. "What the hell happened?" I opened my mouth to speak and whispered.

"What?"

I did it again, and he leaned closer, holding onto the side rail.

I whispered, "Up yours."

I pushed the button.

There was a sharp crack and a flash, and Stamper flew across the room as if he'd been slapped aside by a giant hand. I let go of the button and got out of the handcuff faster than Houdini. I scuttled across the floor to Stamper and was sorry to find he was still breathing.

I rifled his pockets and found his keyring. I had to move fast. Rick would be back soon, and who knew who he'd bring with him. I hauled myself into the wheelchair and made for the door. The Mayview ran like a racehorse. I slowed for a corner and nearly ran headlong into Number 2 and Number 5. I zipped between them, and they stood staring after me, mouths open.

I reached the drafty corridor and followed it to the roll-up steel door of a freight elevator. To the right was a control panel. Stamper's ring had a chrome-plated tubular key that fit the lock. A twist of the wrist and the door rolled upward. I was in the elevator and about to press UP when Stamper and a couple of his friends came running into the corridor. Stamper was one hard-assed bastard, all I can say.

Time for the abacus beads. I threw the works into the corridor and they went under everybody's feet, sending all three sprawling. The door rolled down and it was almost shut when a hand with an automatic snaked through the opening at the bottom. By the size of the hand, I knew it was Stamper. He fired shots wildly, slugs ricocheting off the walls of the car.

I had no choice.

I pushed UP.

Alarms sounded. Lights flashed. The car rose. The pistol went empty. The arm rose with the car. I heard shouting, I heard screaming, then I heard silence.

I was sure there were other ways to get out of the Bunker, and people would be using them. The elevator rose pretty fast and at the top, I held my breath as the door opened. I half expected to be staring down a gun barrel, but no. I would have pried the pistol out of Stamper's detached hand, but I had no bullets.

Under the face of my chronometer was a quarter-sized wafer of plastique and a micro detonator. I stuck it on the elevator control box and tripped the switch. I rolled out of the elevator, and as the control box blew,

I nearly collided with a twenty-foot fiberglass clown.

The clown was standing beside a full-sized carousel. My guess was right. I was in the middle of an amusement park. I recognized Chuckles, the iconic mascot of Happyville, twelve miles south of St. Jacques.

There had to be a pay phone somewhere close. I had no quarters, but I could call collect. I was in the middle of looking when I heard a voice shout, "There he is, behind the Tilt-A-Whirl!"

Gunshots from behind me. Then gunshots from the opposite direction. I was caught in the middle of a crossfire. I slammed the joystick and the chair took off. I was going great til I hit a curb and the chair flipped over, wheels spinning in the air. I landed face down in the gravel. The gunfire stopped in a minute.

Bobbing flashlights. One in my face. "Here!"

I figured I was done, but then another voice. "Doc, are you okay?" I was never so glad to hear your voice, Cap.

The rest is from your end.

•••

Fielding leaned back in his chair. "When I heard your message on the tape from Christine's answering machine, I knew what to do. I called members of my old team, and in no time we were ready to roll."

"How did you know you were under Happyville, Ernie?" Christine asked.

"I heard the carousel and figured it had to be an amusement park."

"But Happyville?"

Doc shrugged. "It was the closest one. I figured they couldn't have taken me too far away. I rolled the dice."

"What better place to hide an underground hideout?" Cap said. "It's out of the city, there's noise all day and into the night, and there's enough electrical access to supply the place. No one would notice trucks delivering supplies and machinery."

Christine scribbled the comment on her pad. "After Doc told you where the elevator shaft was, what happened next?"

"The team and I rappelled down the shaft and went in shooting. Lady Python spent her money outfitting the workshop and came up short on security. It was a rout. We had to blow the door off the shop, and we got inside just in time to see the Worm disappear through the floor. It was throwing dirt ten feet behind it."

"Lady Python was in it?"

Fielding nodded. "With her hencher Walter. We couldn't chase them because the damned machine backfilled its tunnel as it went."

"History repeats itself," Doc said, which earned him a raised eyebrow from Fielding.

"So they got away?"

"Yes and no," Doc said. "They got out of the lab, but I jiggered the Worm so its power shut down in five minutes. They're out there somewhere, six feet under, or sixty."

Christine shuddered. "How awful. To be buried alive."

"Lady P. got what she deserved, but I feel bad about Walter," Doc admitted. "He wasn't an evil sort, but he was an up-and-comer. I figure the world is better off without two of me."

"Amen," Cap said.

"Are you going after the Worm, Cap?" Christine asked. "You could follow the excavation."

"We may. It would be a lot of work and expense, but a device like that could be useful in the future — with a little expert help, right, Doc?"

But Ernie Voskovec didn't answer. His chin was on his chest. He was sleeping peacefully and dreaming of Debbie and her begonias.

THE END

ABOUT OUR CREATORS

WRITER—CREATOR

GREG HATCHER – (1961-2021) Began his writing career in 1992. He was a contributing editor at WITH magazine for over a decade and during that time was a three-time winner of the Higher Goals Award for children's writing; once for fiction and twice for non-fiction. Following that he did a weekly column for Comic Book Resources as one of the rotating features on the Comics Should Be Good! blog for eleven years. He also did a weekly column on pop culture for Atomic Junk Shop. He taught writing in the Young Authors classes offered as part of the Communities-In-Schools Afterschool Arts Program in west Seattle, for students in the 6th through the 12th grade. A fan of pulp fiction ever since he discovered the Doc Savage paperback reprints from Bantam Books in the 1970s. Greg contributed a number of action-adventure stories to various 'new pulp' anthologies. Likewise a lifelong mystery fan, he also wrote Nero Wolfe pastiches for the Wolfe Pack Gazette and several Sherlock Holmes adventures for the Airship 27 CONSULTING DETECTIVE series. At the time of his death, he lived in Burien, Washington, with his wife Julie, their cat Magdalene, and ten thousand books and comics.

WRITER—WRAP UP

FRED ADAMS, JR. is a retired Penn State University English Professor who spends his days writing pulp fiction and his nights working as a singer-songwriter. His Sam Dunne novel *Dead Man's Melody* was nominated as Pulp Novel of the Year in 2017's Pulp Factory Awards, and his Smith Brothers novel *The Eye of Quang-Chi* was nominated for the same award in 2018. His titles include *Hitwolf* 1 and 2, *Six Gun Terrors* vols. 1, 2, and 3, and *C.O. Jones: Mobsters and Monsters, Skinners,* and *The Damned and the Doomed.* His original Sherlock Holmes anthology *The Affair of the Chronic Argonaut* was recently published by Pro Se Press. Forthcoming titles from Airship 27 include *C.O. Jones: Home Front, Six Gun Terrors 4: The Town Killers,* a Sam Dunne Mystery, *Blood is the New Black,* and *Holster Full of Death,* a Dead Sheriff novel. He lives in Mount Pleasant, Pennsylvania in "perpetual terror of boredom."

Visit Fred's website at http://drphreddee.com/author

INTERIOR ILLUSTRATIONS

ROB DAVIS - began his professional art career doing illustrations for role-playing games in the late 1980s. Not long after he began lettering and inking, then penciling comics for several of small black and white comics publishers- most notably for Eternity Comics (which eventually became part of Malibu Comics in the 1990s) on their book SCIMIDAR with writer R.A. Jones. Branching out to other black and white publishers and eventually working at both DC and Marvel Rob worked on likeness-intensive comics like comics adaptations of TV shows QUANTUM LEAP and STAR TREK's many incarnations, mostly on the DEEP SPACE NINE comics for Malibu. At Marvel he worked on the comics adaptation of the Saturday morning cartoon PIRATES OF DARK WATER. After the comics industry implosion in the late 1990's Rob picked up work on video games, advertising illustration, and T-shirt design as well as some small press comics like ROBYN OF SHERWOOD for Caliber. Rob continues to do the occasional self-published comic book as well as publisher and designer for his small-press production REDBUD STUDIO COMICS. Rob is Art Director, Designer, and Illustrator for the New Pulp production outfit AIRSHIP 27 partnered with writer/editor Ron Fortier. He is also working with independent comics publisher SILVERLINE COMICS on future projects. Rob has twice been the recipient of the PULP FACTORY AWARD for "Best Interior Illustrations" for his work on SHERLOCK HOLMES: CONSULTING DETECTIVE. Now retired from "real work", he lives in central Missouri with his wife, their two adult children and their granddaughter.

COVER ARTIST

CHRIS KOHLER - Comics, and the creation of such, have been an obsession for most of my life. Many years had been spent trying to be the next John Byrne (or the next Sal Buscema...) while floundering for some direction and style to go along with the passion. Several more years were spent doing everything *but* drawing.

Finally, at age 30, there was a synergy between the discipline required to draw and the joy felt due to drawing. Since then, a couple of hundred pages of comics or so have been born between short stories for small press groups such as Hidden Agenda Press, Approbation Comics, and commissioned pieces done via eBay and DeviantArt.

From 2009-2013, I worked with writer Daniel VanderMolen on my largest work to date (over 80 pages), a zombie strip called *Portland Underground* (www.pdxunderground.net). Another couple of years were spent creating 32 pages of EC-style shorts with writer Larry King (no relation!), to be published at a later date under the title of '*Tales of Woe*'.

In addition to small press & webcomic work, I've been doing interior illustrations for New Pulp publications such as Van Plexico's entire *Sentinels* novel series (8 books so far), and a couple of one-off collections such as *Blackthorn* and *The Many Worlds of Ulysses King*.

SIX-GUNS AND SORCERY!

In 1868, six people sought refuge at a hidden enclave in the high desert country of eastern Oregon; A brilliant female doctor dying of a rare disease; A Confederate deserter; Two refugees from a lynch mob; A former slave; A womanizing shootist. These were the first acolytes of Stonegarden Abbey, learning the secrets of Hermetic magic under the tutelage of the mysterious prophet Ezekiel Reardon. But Ezekiel had an agenda of his own, and their time at Stonegarden ended in fire and tragedy.

Those left alive thought the tragedy was behind them. But the dark power they believed was gone and buried with Ezekiel only slept, and it is awakening now, ten years later. The survivors of Stonegarden must return to the ruined Abbey when they are called to rescue one of their own, a woman they had thought long dead. With the help of a teenage half-breed Native girl, these broken people must reclaim their old skills and find the strength within themselves to save their fallen sister Anne-Marie from an ancient evil... and the fate of the Earth itself might well hang in the balance.